While We Waited

by Tammy Falkner

Night Shift Publishing

For Peggy and Katie

Tag

There are five of them. I did my homework. Five sisters.

I watched them for weeks before I ever dreamed of approaching them. I know where they go and who they see. I know what their work schedules look like. I even know when they have their periods.

Yeah, I might have looked through their trash a time or two, trying to find out as much as I can before I make my move. And it wasn't easy, with all the security they have. It's like walking up on the White House at times. But I did it.

Now I finally know enough to tell them I'm here.

My biological sisters are the easy ones. They call themselves Star and Wren, but when I knew them they were Jessica and Jenny. They now have the last name of Vasquez. But they will always be Taggerts, no matter how far they travel, how famous they get, or how much they change. No matter how much money they make, they will still be my sisters. My blood.

The others are more of a mystery. There's Peck, and she's the drummer. She just married Sam Reed, the reality TV star and retired pro football player, and they are about to have a baby. She has a really bad speech impairment, and she struggles to talk in public. Just hearing her try to talk on TV makes me cringe for her. Well, more for me than for her. But still.

Then there's Lark. She's the keyboard player. She's also a self-professed germ freak and she wears long elbow-length gloves everywhere she goes. But I have a feeling the gloves are about more than just germs. And I have a bigger feeling that she doesn't want anyone to know it. She's not a germ freak. Something happened to her and she hides it behind fabric and color. I can relate. I hide my past too. I hide it really well. So well that I'm not even sure who I am most days.

Then there's Finch. Fin. Finny, they call her. She's lead guitarist in their band. She's also famous for her one-night stands. She's as famous for them as she is for her music. And her music is pretty darn fabulous. She's tiny, but curvy, and watching her butt shake as she walks down the street makes me want to stick my tongue in all her wet places every time I see her. But I have to shove my wants to the side.

I have an image I've cultivated. A face I show to the rest of the world, and it's the face I have to show my sisters so they'll let me in.

I iron my button-down shirt and shake it out in front of the motel mirror. I spent my last thirty dollars on this room, just so that I could get ready to go to them. I pull my jeans on and slide my feet into some sneakers. I bought all this stupid stuff at Goodwill for less than four dollars. Then I spent eight quarters washing it at the Laundromat. I button my shirt up high and put on the blue tie, which is already threatening to choke me.

I pick up my duffle bag and glance around the room to be sure I didn't forget anything. Nothing here is mine. I step into the bathroom and grab the free soap and shampoo samples. No idea when I'll see a shower again, so I might need them. I can wash my hair in a rest stop bathroom, if push comes to shove. I stuff them into the front pocket of the duffle bag.

Now it's time to go and find my sisters. I know where they live. I've watched them come and go for weeks, so I know their schedules as well as they do. They're not touring right now since Peck is about to have a baby.

I wait for residents to go into their apartment building, and I slip through the door just before it closes. I pretend like I belong here, even though this swanky building with its fancy doorman isn't anything like where I come from. I walk beside one of the building's residents and pretend to talk to her so the doorman will think I'm with her. I don't want him to stop me.

The woman regards me with interest. She likes me. I can tell. But I'm on a mission. I ignore her when she keeps talking. I got what I wanted from her, which was entry into the building. She's expendable, and she's aware of it. She flounces off the elevator at her stop and I breathe a sigh of relief.

I go up a few more levels, stop outside their door, and drop my bag to the floor. I force myself to halt and take a deep breath. The door opens and it's like falling back in time.

"Jess," I breathe.

She startles and stumbles into the doorframe. I reach out a hand to catch her, but she jerks herself back at the last minute.

I smile at her. "Hi," I say.

She slams the door in my face. The cool rush of air smacks hard against me and I force myself not to throw open the door and chase her into the room.

I knock. No one comes to the door. I know she's in there. There's not another exit, not that I'm aware of. I knock again and lean my forehead against the cool metal. "Please," I whisper.

The door flies open and I nearly stumble into the room. I catch myself on the doorjamb and look at Jess's face.

"Hi," I say again, like an idiot.

"Go away," she says. Then she ducks under my arm and passes me in the hallway, slamming the door shut behind her.

"Wait," I call. "Can we talk?"

She turns back to face me and points her finger at my nose. "Talk? *Talk?*" She shrieks the last word. "After all this time, you suddenly want to *talk?*"

I nod. "Yes. Please."

"No." She turns and stalks down the corridor.

"Come on, Jess—"

She turns back and advances on me so fast that I retreat, my back striking the door. "My name is Star. And you would know that if you had returned any of the letters I sent to you over the years, you jackass."

"What letters?" I never got any letters.

"I wrote you every day for a year, you piece of shit excuse for a brother."

Well, at least she acknowledges that I'm family. That's a start.

"I never got any letters," I say. I hold up my hands like I'm surrendering to the cops.

She freezes. But then she lets out a hiss of breath and starts to shake her head. "Fuck you," she says. She turns and walks away. I chase after her, but she leaves me standing there in the hallway. The elevator doors close behind her, and I think about racing down the stairs so I can intercept her, but I have a feeling that won't help me.

Well. I messed that up.

I walk back to her doorway and sink down onto the floor and cross my legs. I'll wait. I can't give up on this. I have too much at stake. If I wait here, she'll have to talk to me eventually, right?

It's two hours later when the elevator dings and I hear footsteps in the corridor. I sit up. It's not her, though. My heart clutches in my chest, because it's Jenny. "Jen?"

I lumber to my feet, my ass sore from sitting on the floor.

Jenny freezes and stares at me. "Tag?" Then she breaks her gaze and looks at my duffle bag, her eyes skittering from place to place.

"It's me, Jenny," I say softly.

She sticks her key in the lock and swings the door open, then nods for me to follow her. My heart rejoices. I'm in the fucking door. So far so good.

She lays her things on the kitchen counter. "What are you doing here?" she asks. She looks like she has the weight of the world on her shoulders.

"I wanted to see how you're both doing," I say quietly. "Are you okay?"

She snorts. "You're asking that now? After all this time?" Her eyes narrow. "Why do you care?"

"You're my sister, Jenny," I remind her. I need for her to remember that. I need *them*.

"My name is Wren. Wren Vasquez. My father's name is Emilio and my mother's name is Marta. I'm twenty-four years old and my sisters are Star, Finny, Lark, and Peck. I don't have a brother. Not anymore." She turns and takes a cold drink from the fridge. She doesn't offer me one, but I'm okay with that.

"Wren," I say. Her new name sounds foreign on my tongue. "It has been so long," I tell her.

Looking into her face is like staring my mother in the eye. They look so much alike that it's disturbing. "You look like Mom," I blurt out.

Her eyes fill with tears and she blinks them back. "Tag," she breathes. "Damn it. Why now?"

"I'm in trouble." I didn't mean to say it, but I did. "Lots of trouble. Back home." I scrub my hands down my face.

"What kind of trouble?"

"The really bad kind." I look everywhere but at her. "I was hoping I might be able to stay with you for a few days maybe." A few days…or just long enough to get you to trust me and give me money so that I can take care of something back home.

I hold my breath and wait for a response. But none comes. "Or maybe just long enough to save up a few dollars?" I need to put the fact that I need money directly in her face.

"Star won't like it," she says.

I wince. "I already saw her."

Her eyes narrow at me. "What happened?"

"She pretty much told me to fuck off."

She laughs. "That sounds like Star."

"So, can I stay?" I hold my breath. I need this. I *really* need it.

"Put your stuff in Peck's old room," she says, pointing to a door down the hallway. Her phone dings and she smiles down at it. "I have to go to the hospital," she says as I come back down the hallway after dropping off my bag.

"Hospital? Are you okay?"

She waves a breezy hand in the air. "I'm fine. But Peck's having a baby. We need to get there." She motions for me to follow her.

"Do you just want me to wait here for you?"

"Dude, I know you're my brother, but I'm not leaving you alone in our apartment."

"I understand." I nod and follow her to the door.

At the last minute, she turns back to face me. "If you hurt Star, or anyone else in my family, I will make you regret it. Do you understand?"

My heart stutters, but I nod.

They're going to hate me when this is all over.

She's kind of quiet in the cab on the way to the hospital. She texts a lot and makes a few calls, cursing when she doesn't get an answer. She makes some small talk with me but she doesn't really say much. Finally, she pays the driver and we get out. I run a hand through my hair.

She laughs. "You look fine," she says.

"Will your adoptive parents be here?"

She nods. "Yep. You'll like them, though. They're awesome."

We stop at the reception desk and they send us to maternity, where Jenny—I mean *Wren*—asks for Peck's room. They show us to a waiting room, and we walk in, but it's empty except for Jess—I mean *Star*—and a man in a wheelchair.

Star jumps to her feet when she sees me. "What's *he* doing here?"

Wren glares at her. "Where the fuck have you been? I've been trying to find you everywhere." She holds up her phone and points at Star's.

"Why did you bring him here?" Star asks. "He doesn't belong here."

Wren puts her hands on her hips. "Yes, he does."

People start filing down the hallway, and I recognize some of the girls from Fallen from Zero, the band my sisters belong to. I also recognize Star and Wren's adoptive parents. I've seen them in publicity photos. Her dad glares at me but he doesn't say anything. He knows who I am, though. That much is obvious.

Star gets up and walks down the hallway. She's pissed.

"Well, that went well," Wren says as she flops into a chair. She points to the guy in the wheelchair, then at me. "Oh, this is our brother, Tag. Tag, this is Josh. Josh works at the tattoo shop I was telling you about, with the Reeds." She'd mentioned the Reeds briefly when she was prattling on about nothing in the cab.

I shake his hand. "Nice to meet you," I say. He has ink across his knuckles and pretty much everywhere else.

"Aren't you going to see the baby?" Josh asks.

"Is it here?" Wren cries.

Josh nods and smiles. Wren shrieks and gets to her feet, then runs down the hallway.

I sit with Josh for a minute. The silence wraps around us like a warm wool blanket. It's heavy and oppressive. "Where are you from, man?" he finally asks.

"From the past," I say. "And apparently I should have stayed there." But I need this. I need my sisters in so many ways.

"What brings you to New York?"

I shrug. "I needed a change." *And a lot of money to pay off a girl so I can get a baby.*

"So you thought looking up long-lost sisters was the way to go?"

I laugh, but it comes out sounding pretty insincere. "It was now or never, you know? I needed to be in the city. I just didn't expect to walk into a mess."

"Some call it a baby. Some call it a mess." He holds his hands up like he's weighing two things, lowering one and raising the other.

"Yeah, Wren filled me in on the way here. Babies are pretty special. A gift from God." I find that people trust a God-fearing individual. So, I am one. Or at least I want him to think I am. My own faith is currently on shaky ground. But he doesn't need to know that.

"I'm going to go and find Star," he suddenly says. He starts to roll down the hallway and I stay in my seat. My sisters have to walk by me in order to exit, so I wait.

"See you later, man," I say.

I wait. And wait. And wait…and when no one returns I'm worried that they left without me.

I get up and go down the hallway, peering into doorways until I see Josh in his wheelchair inside a room. I knock on the door and stick my head inside. "Can I join you?" I ask. I flinch inside, worried they'll say no.

Star sits up and says, "No, you may not."

"Oh, shut it, Star." Wren motions me into the room and makes introductions. Sam Reed, who I recognize from TV, looks curious. And Peck doesn't look like she appreciates my presence at all.

After a few minutes of awkward silence, Peck yawns. Josh says, "I'm going to go home so you guys can get some rest." Sam takes his baby from Josh, who had been holding him.

"Where's *he* going to stay?" Star asks, nodding toward me.

Wren heaves a sigh. "He's going to stay in Peck's old room for a few days."

"No, he is not!" Star jumps to her feet and punches her hands into her hips. "*No!*"

Wren closes her eyes and massages her forehead. "The room is just sitting there empty. He doesn't have anywhere to go."

"And this is our problem why?"

"Because he shares our DNA!" Wren yells. The baby startles and Sam growls at them both. But inside, I rejoice because it has been a long time since anyone has taken up for me.

"Knock it off," Sam warns.

"Why can't he get a hotel room?" Star asks, her voice growing quiet.

"Because he doesn't have any money!" Wren whisper-hisses back.

"Money," Star bites out. "That's what this is about."

Yep. She pegged me in two seconds.

"He's going home with us. That's all there is to it." Wren clenches her teeth.

"Then I'm not." Star stares her down.

Wren sighs. She glares at our sister. "If that's how you want it."

"Fine." Star leans over and kisses Peck on the forehead, whispers in her ear, and then kisses Sam's cheek. "I'll see you tomorrow." Then Star walks out of the room.

Sam nods his head subtly at Josh, and Josh follows her out, rolling in her wake.

"That didn't go very well," I say. "I should go and get her." I get to my feet.

"You better not," Peck warns.

I jerk my thumb in the direction she went. "But she's leaving."

"Let her go," Sam says. "Josh will take care of her. He's been taking care of her all night."

Wren grins. "Oh, do tell," she says.

Sam starts to tell us about Star dancing on a piano, so drunk she could barely walk. My conscience prickles a little, since I know I caused that.

"Star never gets drunk like that," Wren says quietly. She looks worried.

"Josh will take care of her," Sam says again. He doesn't look worried at all. In fact, he winks at his wife and she grins at him, rolling her eyes.

"I feel bad that she's not going home. And it's all because of me," I say quietly.

"She'll come home when she's ready," Peck says.

The question is, will she be ready in time for me take care of things back home? I need for them to love me and to trust me. Then I need for them to give me money, and I can't get them to do any of that if they're not around.

***

I haven't seen Star since I got here. She refused to come back to the apartment, and she has been away the three days I've been here. But Wren has been here. All it took was some reminiscing. Bam. Got her.

"Do you remember the yellow house on Chestnut Street?" I ask her.

Wren blinks her eyes furiously. "Yes, I remember."

It was the house we lived in when Mom and Dad died. "Dad taught you how to ride that old pink bike on the sidewalk out front."

"I remember." Her voice is thick and tight. "That was before…"

"Before they died," I finish quietly. I force out a laugh. "You scraped your knee when you fell off the bike and you wanted to quit, but Dad wouldn't let you."

She chuckles. It's a watery sound. "He made me get back on it and stay on it until I could ride it around the block."

"Then they couldn't get you to come inside for supper," I remind her. My breath catches at the look of devastation on her face. But I push on. "You wanted to stay outside all night."

"The streetlights came on and I wanted to keep riding."

"Dad sat on the porch and counted your laps around the block."

A tear finally falls over her lashes and my gut twists. "I miss them," she whispers.

"You got a good family," I remind her. Not like the one I got.

"We didn't at first," she blurts out. Then she looks like she wants to take it back.

I drop the fork I'm holding and it clatters to the tabletop. "What?"

"Our first foster family…" She shakes her head. "Never mind."

"Tell me," I say.

"You don't want to know."

"I do." It can't be as bad as the hell I went through. "Tell me."

"He was a pedophile, and she was clueless." She closes her eyes. "Star bore the brunt of it."

I suddenly want to throw up. "*What?*"

She nods. It's a quick jerk. "Social Services took us out of there and we went to a group home. It was better." She smiles at me. "Then we met Marta and Emilio and they adopted all of us."

"I didn't know," I manage to respond. I can barely breathe, much less speak. No wonder she hates me.

"Star wrote to you all the time. She kept thinking you were going to come and rescue us." She laughs, but there's no humor in it. None at all. "That's why she's not here. She's still a little sore over it."

"If I had known–"

But she holds up a hand and waves it to stop me. "You were a kid."

"I was glad you didn't end up where I went," I blurt out. I want to bite it back as soon as it comes out of my mouth. But it hangs there in the air between us.

She blinks her big brown eyes at me. "Why?"

"It wasn't good." I cough into my fist. "*He* wasn't good."

"*He* was family," she rushes to remind me.

"There was a reason why Dad didn't talk to him. Think back. Do you remember Dad ever having anything nice to say about him?"

She shakes her head. "Not really. But there's a lot I don't remember."

"He wasn't nice or good or kind. And he's no family of mine. Or yours, for that matter." I get up and start to clear the table. "Just thinking about him makes me sick."

"What happened?" she asks from behind me.

"I don't want to talk about it."

"Why not?"

I take a deep breath. "He got paid by the state to keep me." I don't say more, hoping she'll draw her own awful conclusions. "I was like their servant. I took care of their younger kids and kept their house clean." And I took the beatings for the ones who were smaller than me.

"You weren't an only child, at least," she prompts. She's looking for a happy ending, but I can assure her there isn't one. Not in my uncle's house.

She sounds so optimistic I almost hate to shatter her illusions. "I took care of everyone. I cooked and cleaned and changed diapers and put the kids on the bus. I nursed fevers and soothed nightmares." I shiver at the thought of it. "And then they sent me to my room, when my chores were done, while they were a family and I had no one."

"We didn't know…"

"No one did." I shrug and force out a laugh I don't feel. Just going back to those days in my head makes my skin crawl. "When I was nineteen, I met a man who worked at a church. He had a daughter, and she made everything better. She helped me. We were the same age. Julia." Just the thought of Julia makes my heart speed up a beat. She's why I have to go back. She's why I'm here at all.

"That's good," Wren says.

I force my own memories to the back of my mind. "Do you remember the time that you and Star decided to build a tree house?" I ask. I force her to slip back into the memories, and I go with her. And I'm happy for a little while, as I bask in the glow that is my family.

Suddenly, I realize that I've had too much to drink. My emotions are sitting directly below the surface of my skin. They're not hidden down deep in my soul where I usually keep them. They're floating just below my sanity, and they're peeking through.

"I need to go to bed," Wren says. She presses her beer toward me. She cracked it open but never drank any of it.

I have already had a six pack or so. I'm not drunk, but I'm losing my inhibitions and I'm sober enough to know it. I push the beer back toward her.

"I can't," she says on a laugh. "Not possible." She narrows her eyes at me though, and I immediately worry. Did I say something I shouldn't have said? Did I lie? Does she know it? "I want to give you something," she says. She digs into her purse and pulls out a blue faux-leather bank book. She slides it toward me. "I set this up for you today."

"What is it?" I ask. But inside my heart is leaping.

She winces. "I kind of went through your wallet to get your information for the account."

"Oh." I immediately wonder what else she found.

"I wasn't really snooping. Just trying to figure out how to set this up for you."

"Okay." My heart is pounding. She just made all my dreams come true and she doesn't even know it. She thinks she just did a good deed.

"I want you to stay. I want you to stay long enough for Star to get to talk to you at least, once she gets over the hurt. But I understand if you can't." Her voice is quiet but strong. "No matter what, I want you to be taken care of. I want you to know you're loved."

My heart leaps into my throat. It wasn't supposed to happen like this. I was supposed to trick them into loving me. They weren't supposed to just do it. I push the bank book back toward her. "No, I can't take it," I say.

"It's not much. Just a nest egg." She comes toward me and lays her hand on the top of my head. She gives my head a shove and kisses my forehead just like our mom used to do. It was more like getting assaulted with affection when Mom did it, and we all loved it so much. So having her do it brings tears to my eyes. "I'm glad you're here," she whispers to me. Then she goes into her room and closes the door softly behind her.

I drop my head to the tabletop and bite back a sob. I can't cry. I can't. I haven't shed a tear since I went to live with *him*—at least not where anyone could see me. I open up the bank book and see a blank set of checks with my name on them. And there's a total written at the top of the register.

She put fifty thousand dollars into an account for me.

For *me*. Holy shit. Fifty thousand dollars…

I lay my head on the cool tabletop and roll my forehead across the surface. If I were a better man, I wouldn't take it. But I'm not. I'm desperate.

A key jangles on the other side of the door and I lift my head, swipe beneath my eyes, and try to pretend like my emotions aren't slapping me in the face like lightning in a summer storm. I'm probably failing at it, but I do try.

The door opens and Fin comes in. She's wearing a pair of black jeans that hug her ass and a black leather jacket. She's bad-ass. And beautiful. And I'm a little bit drunk.

She trips over the doormat and grabs hold of the wall. She giggles. Oh, hell. She's tipsy too.

"Hey," she says as she tosses her keys onto the counter with a clatter.

"Hey," I mutter back. I roll the bank book in my hand, trying to figure out if I can take it.

"Where is everybody?"

I nod toward Wren's room. "Wren just went to bed. Lark's not home yet. And Star is at Josh's apartment, still."

She nods and shrugs out of her leather jacket. She's wearing a thin camisole and no bra. Her nipples press hard against the sheer fabric and I have to force myself not to look. She bends over and looks into the fridge. "What happened to all the beer?"

I pick up my can and drain the last of it. "Drank it," I murmur.

She gets a bottle of water and sits down across from me. "Bad night?"

I shake my head. "Good night. You?" I arch an eyebrow at her.

She shrugs. "Good as any other. I'm a little bit drunk." She holds up her thumb and forefinger about an inch apart.

I laugh. "Oh, good. Me too."

She goes into her room and comes back with a guitar. I watch her as she goes to the couch and plops down on it. She settles the acoustic guitar in her lap so that it's facing up and she starts to pluck at the strings. A melody jumps into the air and dances in front of me.

"That's really good," I say. I'm drawn to the music almost as much as I'm drawn to the girl. I get up and go into the living room. "Can I sit?"

She shrugs. I plop down on the other end of the couch and watch her. She plucks and hums and plucks some more and then she stops and writes something down.

"Are you writing music?" I ask.

"Something like that," she murmurs.

"It's really good. Does it have words?"

"Yeah," she says, as she chews on the tip of her pen. A lock of dark hair falls into her face and she blows it to the side. I reach over and brush it back when it falls again. She startles, jerked out of her musical trance, and she stares at me. "You want to hear the words?" she asks, her voice quiet, almost fearful.

"Yes." I can't think of anything I'd like more.

She starts to sing. It's tentative and wary and so fucking beautiful that she steals my breath. She sings about heartbreak and shame and lust and love and hurt, and under it all…there's beauty. Just…sheer beauty.

When she stops playing, I realize that I haven't even breathed, so I take in a breath and fill my aching lungs. "That was amazing." I sigh.

"How drunk are you?"

I shake my head. "Not *very*."

"You should drink another." She nods her head toward the kitchen.

"Why?"

She stares hard at me. "Because I want to find out what makes you tick."

I'm not even sure I *do* tick. I kind of just exist. Ever since I got the call from Julia that she didn't want our baby, that she wanted out, I've felt like someone pushed the pause button on my life.

"What makes *you* tick, Finny?" I ask.

She snorts. But it's an adorable sound and I find myself grinning. And it's not just because I'm drunk. "Sex," she says. "Sex makes me tick."

I choke on my own spittle. "Beg your pardon?"

She laughs. "I like to have sex, Tag. Lots of sex."

"Okay…" I say slowly.

"You're going to go all gospel on me and tell me that good girls don't have sex with random strangers, right?" She shakes her head and points her finger at me. "But I have news for you. I can do whatever I want with my body. I can fuck anybody I want."

I cringe at her choice of words.

"Oh, you just gave me *the look*," she says.

"What look?"

"The I'm-judging-you look."

"I did not."

"Yes, you did. You think it's wrong for a woman to like sex."

I shake my head. "I didn't say that."

"Yes, you did. Your body language said it." She starts to pluck at the guitar again.

"Really, I don't care who you have sex with." I worry a loose thread on my jeans. I don't like this conversation. "I think I'm going to bed." I set my hands on my knees and start to push myself up.

"Want some company?" she asks.

I freeze. "What?"

"I have two rules," she states. She starts to tick items off on her fingers. "One, I don't sleep with anyone more than once. And two, you have to get out of my bed when we're done."

I frown. "Where's the fun in that?"

"Um, your dick…my vagina…lots of pounding. Fun. *There's* the fun in that."

I shake my head. I've only been with one woman in my life, and she dumped me months ago. But being with her forged a connection. And the connection wasn't necessarily in the dick-to-vagina pounding sessions, as Finny so unromantically put it. It was in the quiet moments after the sex. It was when she laid her head on my chest and dragged her fingers back and forth through the sparse dusting of hair. It was when we woke up stuck together with sweat between us. It was the beat of her heart while she lay on top of me. It was the way she wrapped around me, encompassing my heart with the same kind of heat she wrapped around my dick when I was inside her.

"You're thinking about sex, aren't you?" Finny asks.

"Not really," I admit. "I was thinking about intimacy."

She snorts again. "Sex is so much better than intimacy."

I shake my head. "I don't believe you."

"I'll prove it to you." She sets the guitar to the side and gets up on her knees. She nibbles on her lower lip as she walks on her hands and knees across the few inches of sofa between us.

I fall back against the couch as she climbs into my lap. "What are you doing?"

"If you have to ask, I'm doing it wrong," she says. She grins, and it makes me want to grin with her.

I take her shoulders and push her back. "What about my sisters?"

"What about them?" She nips my lower lip between her teeth. Then she sucks it into her mouth to ease the sting, and it shoots straight to my dick. "I don't usually ask their permission when I want to fuck somebody."

I point to my chest. "You want to fuck *me?*"

She laughs and grinds her pussy against me. "I think that part is obvious."

"Why?" I ask. I hold her face so I can keep her from kissing me, and stare into her eyes.

She straddles me and presses her breasts against me. "Because you're here," she replies.

"Oh," I say. That's her only requirement?

She sits back. "I thought I was getting a vibe from you..." she says doubtfully, searching my face. "Was I wrong?"

"Hell no!" She's right. She has already intrigued me. And she's beautiful. So beautiful. But this can't happen. It just can't.

She grins. "So you *do* want to fuck me."

Damn. The heat of her words shoots straight to my dick.

I kiss her. I can't help it. Her pussy is hot and it's just on the other side of my zipper and she smells so damn good. My head is a little swimmy, but my dick isn't. He's ready.

I jerk my head back when a thought comes into my head. "Is it weird that you're my sisters' sister?"

"Dude, we are so *not* related," she says. "But if you feel weird about it…" She sits back, and I feel the loss of her immediately. She scoots back to her side of the couch.

"Don't go," I protest.

She smiles and runs her thumbs below the straps of her camisole, then suddenly pulls it down beneath her breasts. She looks toward Wren's room and chews on her lower lip. But I can't look at her face. All I see is tits. Beautiful, perfect round tits with perfect hard nipples. I lick my lips. I want to taste them.

"I'm going to bed," she says. She gives me a look over her shoulder as she walks away from me. She goes into her room and leaves the door cracked.

I drag a hand through my hair. Holy shit. I adjust my junk because I'm so hard that I can barely stand it.

She comes back to her doorway and leans on the doorjamb. She's naked. Completely stark fucking naked. "You coming?" she asks quietly.

I nod. I get up and go to her, because I feel like she's a magnet and I'm metal and she's pulling me toward her without even trying.

I step into the room, close the door behind me, and she sits on the edge of the bed. She hooks her fingers in the belt loops of my jeans and pulls me toward her.

"Wait," I say.

She lays her forehead against my stomach and I can feel her breath against my dick, hot through the fabric. God, she's turning me on.

I've never had casual sex, though.

"So, you don't cuddle?" I ask. I shouldn't even be in here, but she's here and she's all but kissing the button of my jeans.

"No. No cuddling."

"What if I want to cuddle?"

"What if I want to just fuck you?" She lifts her face and stares up at me. "It doesn't have to be more than that. Just one time."

"Your rules," I mutter.

"Yes. Are you in or are you out?"

"I've never…" I scrub a hand down my face.

"You've never…?" She waits for my answer as she pops the button of my jeans.

"I've never…had sex with someone I don't love." There. I said it. I've been with one woman. That's it. And she is now with someone else.

"There's a certain joy in sex with no strings," she says quietly. She lifts the bottom edge of my T-shirt and touches her lips to my tender skin. My dick pulses. I lay my head back and groan. "Finny," I growl.

"You can say no," she says quietly. But her hands grab onto my ass and she pulls me toward her, her lips dancing across my skin.

"You're making it damn hard."

She probes my dick with her fingertips, outlining the ridge of me. "Yep," she says on a giggle. "Remember? It's easy with me. No repeat performances. I won't ask you for flowers. Or for promises. I won't even ask you to hold me after."

"What if I want to?" It's hard to think with her this close to me.

"Want to what?" she murmurs against me. She replaces her tiny kisses with the tip of her tongue, and she licks across my stomach. My dick jumps.

"What if I want to cuddle?" I ask.

She freezes. Her eyes meet mine. "Why?"

Because I seriously need to cuddle. I need for someone to act like they love me, even if it's just for a minute. "I don't know why," I hedge. But I want it more than I want her to take my dick into her mouth. I want it more than I want to be inside her. My existence is a lonely one. And if she's offering to take some of that away for a minute or two, I'll take her up on it. But it can't be just my dick slamming into her vagina. It has to be something I can feel. "I don't know why...but I need it."

She nods. "I'll give you twenty minutes."

"What?"

"After you fuck me, I'll let you stay for twenty minutes. Take it or leave it."

She slowly lowers my zipper. "Take it," I whisper fiercely.

She shoves my jeans and my boxers down in one motion, and then she tears a condom wrapper open with her teeth and rolls the condom down my length. I grit my teeth and try not to come in her hand. It has been a very long time since I've done this. And I've never done *this*. Not like this. Not with someone I don't love.

"Are you sure?" I ask. She was tipsy. "Are you still drunk?"

She shakes her head. "No." She crab-walks naked across the bed, and holds her arms out to me. "Stop being such a girl," she says. She points to my dick. "That," she says, and then she points to her pussy, which is pink and pretty and perfect and right in front of me, "goes here."

I nod and fall on top of her. I'm suddenly completely sober. And I'm entranced. She wraps her legs around me, taking control as she pulls me toward her. "Wait," I say. "Slow down just a little."

She groans and flops her arms out flat on the bed. "You're not one of *them*, are you?"

"One of what?" I ask as I brush her hair back from her face.

"One that wants to rock my world. One that wants to teach me how breathtaking lovemaking can be. One of the stupid people."

"No, I'm not one of them," I say. I stare into her eyes as I press against her heat, sliding in her wetness. I press inside her slowly, afraid I'll hurt her. Afraid I'll do it wrong. Afraid I won't please her.

Her breath hitches and she clutches my hair in her fists. "More," she says.

She jerks my hair, chastising me without words for going too slow. I grab her wrists and press her hands to the bed, holding her in place with my own. I don't want her to take over.

"Stop," I order. I stay still inside her. She pulls at my ass with her feet, but I refuse to move. "Stop," I say again. I bend my head and bite her shoulder and she stares up at me.

She freezes, and I see something move in her eyes. Something needy and vulnerable and wanting.

"I'm not going to let you use me like you use the rest of them," I say, and I rock my hips, sliding deep inside her.

She fights my hands holding hers, and I just squeeze tighter. She laughs. "So you want to *make love* to me?" She rolls her eyes.

I shake my head and then take her nipple into my mouth. It's hot and hard and sweet against my tongue. She tips her hips, trying to get me to move. "No, I want to fuck you." I sink as deep as I can go inside her, and a cry leaves her throat, tickling my ear. "I want to fuck you," I say again. I pull out and slide back in, going as deep as I can go.

If I say *I want to fuck you* a hundred more times, maybe I'll believe it.

She wiggles her fingers. "Let me touch you," she says.

I shake my head. "No."

"Why not?"

"Because you want to take control, and I don't want to give it to you." I pump my hips. She arches to meet me, giving me all of her.

"You want to be in charge," she says on a laugh, and it almost pushes me out of her. I burrow in deep and stop moving.

"No." I shake my head. "I just don't want you to use me like the others. That's all."

"You want to be special." She drops her voice down to a purr. "You're special, baby, just like all the rest."

I pull out of her and flip her over, then smack her ass as I sink inside her from behind.

"Did you just *hit* me?" She stops moving. But her hands are fisted in the sheets, so I know she's not angry. She's turned on. Still.

She arches her back and pushes against me, taking all of me, and I have to grit my teeth and work hard not to come.

I slide my hand beneath her hip and find her pussy. In every porn flick I've ever seen, the guy goes straight for the clit. So, I go for it. She's so wet she's slippery, and I rub her nub. She lays her cheek on the bed and stares out to the side. I know I've found the right spot when her eyes close and her back arches. She pushes her bottom back to meet me. She's so tight like this that I can barely keep from shooting my load inside her. I stop and roll her back over.

"You're going to give a girl whiplash with all this flipping back and forth," she says on a laugh.

"Nope. Just an orgasm," I say. *I hope.* I push her legs open wide and stare down at her.

She laughs. "Oh, you're going to make me come like crazy, right?"

I look up and heave a sigh. "Do you taunt every man you're with like this?"

Her smile fades.

"No wonder no one comes back for seconds," I say. I pull out of her, close her legs, and roll her to the side.

She sits up and her jaw falls open. "Who the fuck do you think—"

I point to my chest. "I'm the guy you're fucking," I say.

"Well, not anymore," she bites out.

"No man in his right mind can take all that mouth," I tell her.

"My mouth just happens to be amazing," she counters. "You want to try that?" But she's already reaching for her robe, so I have a feeling that's off the table.

"Can I tell you something?" My heart is beating like mad.

"Please enlighten me," she replies, her tone pure acid.

"I wanted to have sex with that girl who wrote the beautiful song and then climbed into my lap. She was beautiful and sexy and interesting." And she promised she would cuddle with me after.

She nods. "Then you found out what I'm really like."

"No. That's just it."

She shushes me and glances toward the door like she's afraid someone will hear us, so I try to be quiet.

"That's just it," I whisper fiercely. "I didn't find out what you're really like. I found out how you want to be for all the rest of them." I shake my head. "Never mind."

I pick up my jeans and shake them out.

"Wait," she says quietly. "I don't understand."

I close my eyes and take a deep breath. "It's like you're playing a part. You're working so hard to keep me from seeing you that I can't get close to you at all. That's all."

"I am not—"

"Why did you want to fuck me?"

Her voice is small. "Because you were here."

I nod.

"There's nothing wrong with a woman who just likes to have sex."

"I agree."

She walks by me and I grab her hips. I lift the edge of her robe and look at her ass. "My handprint is on your ass," I say. I bend my head and bite it and she stops breathing.

"I can't believe you hit me."

"Neither can I." I laugh and nibble the curve of her bottom. "You want to try again?" I ask against her skin.

She turns and climbs onto my lap, straddling me. She pumps my dick in her hand and then positions me at her heat. I hold my breath as she slides down my dick, taking me inside.

Her arms wrap around my neck and she sucks my earlobe between her teeth, nibbling gently. I lick across the side of her throat and bite her skin ever so gently. Her pussy trembles around me. "You like that?" I ask.

She doesn't answer, but a hiss escapes her when I bend my head and take her nipple gently between my teeth. I watch her body, listen to her whimper, and realize what she does like just by paying attention.

"I like your dick," she says. She looks into my eyes as she rises and falls.

"I like your pussy," I say. I like it a lot. Too much, because my balls are already trying to crawl up my throat.

"Then you should take a closer look at it." She stops moving and lifts her brows, waiting for me to agree.

I lift her off my dick and flip us over. Her legs fall open and she bites her lower lip between her teeth. Her pussy glistens with wetness and I spread her open with my thumbs. I lean down and blow across her clit. "Am I close enough?" I ask.

Her hips rock and she threads her fingers into my hair, pulling my face closer. I lick across her clit and watch her reaction. She closes her eyes tightly, but she's not making those happy noises. I find her clit and suck hard. She whimpers. Got her.

I slide two fingers into her heat and crook them, looking for the squishy spot I read about in a book. I know when I find it, because I have to hold her hips to the bed. She bucks against my hand and I have to latch on hard to her clit to hang on. Suddenly, she goes still and a cry breaks from her throat, just as her pussy starts to quiver around my fingers. I make her ride it out, working her until she pushes me away.

Her legs are like noodles when I close them and roll her onto her stomach. I cover her body with mine from shoulders to feet, and twine our hands together. She looks up at me, startled, but then she softens and lets me push my way inside. She cries out when I shove my length into her in one hurried stroke.

"I'm sensitive after I come," she whispers.

"I'll be careful," I whisper back. I kiss her softly on her bare shoulder, and her arms bristle with goose bumps. I take her slowly and with care, and she's soft as cotton under me. She turns her head and kisses me, her eyes meeting mine when she pulls back, and there's something in her eyes that I don't completely understand. "You okay?" I ask.

She arches her back and pushes against me and I know then that she's fine. "Can you make me come like this?"

"Can I?" I ask.

I lift her onto her knees and pull her ass back, holding her tightly at her hips, pulling her back to me, pounding hard, harder, harder.

"Jesus," I gasp. "You feel so good. I can't hold off."

"Not yet," she says. She looks at me over her shoulder, and her lips part. "Almost," she breathes.

I nod and screw into her, threading my fingers into the hair at the nape of her neck. I give it a tug and she cries out. I use her hair to turn her head. I want to see her face.

"Now!" she suddenly cries.

I come hard inside the condom, deep inside her, my toes curling with the force of my orgasm, as she shudders, milking me, drawing me in farther and farther. I stop, and her pussy pulls at me until she settles. She lets me slide out and falls against the mattress. I drop on top of her, not ready yet to let her go.

She rolls and I fall down beside her, but then she pulls me to lay my head beneath her breasts. Her hands slide into my hair and she holds my head on her chest, her fingers gently abrading my scalp. "You have twenty minutes to cuddle," she says.

"Cuddling is for douchebags."

She yawns. "You have to get out of my room in nineteen and a half minutes."

"Shut up," I say, stalling. "I need some post-coital comfort."

She laughs and my head rocks on her chest. "Is that anything like cuddling?"

I kiss her belly and lay my face on her soft skin. She strokes my hair, her fingers playing against my scalp. I lift my head, resting my chin on the soft skin of her lower belly. "This is the best part," I tell her.

She snorts. "You keep telling yourself that."

***

Time passes, and she keeps rubbing my scalp. It has been a lot longer than twenty minutes and she hasn't kicked me out yet. But then her hands get tired and heavy against my hair. I don't move immediately. I am enjoying this peacefulness. There's nothing more peaceful than being with a woman who has just had an orgasm or two. I don't want to give this up. This is the part that matters.

A soft snuffling sound escapes her mouth and I know she's asleep. I cautiously sit up.

I have things I need to do. I need to pack. And I need to get out of here before everyone gets up. The bed shifts when I roll, and she reaches for me. I press my lips to the back of her hand and hold it while she settles. Then I get up and pull my clothes on.

I watch her as she lies there completely naked. She's so beautiful. She's tiny and curvy and her long dark hair is spread all over her pillow. I recall the way it felt when I tugged her head back, and my dick jumps. Fuck. I have to get out of here now or I never will.

I pull the covers over her and stare down at her soft face. At a different time, in a different place…I could ask her out. I could try to turn it into something real. But I can't. Not now.

I zip my pants, let myself out of her room, and run straight into Lark, who is coming in the front door.

Her brow arches. "You must have gone in the wrong door," she says. She points toward my room. "Your room is that way."

"Good to know," I mutter, and I go in there.

I pack my things as quickly as I can, then stick my head into the hallway. The apartment is dark except for a light in the kitchen. I carry my duffle bag into the room and stare down at the kitchen table. The bank book. It's why I came here. I have to take it. I can't do what I have to do without it. I pick it up and slip it into my back pocket. She wanted me to have it, so it's not wrong. Right?

I stop outside Finny's door and hesitate for a minute.

"You should go," Lark says from her own doorway.

She startles me and my breath quickens. I nod. "I know," I say quietly.

"It's better this way."

I nod again. "It is."

Lark's door closes and I take a deep breath.

It's time to go. I have to go get my wife and son.

Finny

I stand on the other side of the door and listen to him talk to Lark. I'm still naked and I can smell his sweat on my body.

I grab my robe and slide it on, the silk gliding against the skin he just gave goose bumps. I've been with a lot of men, but I've never had one take over my senses, not like he did. When he laid his head on my chest, I found myself reaching for him, needing to cuddle with him as much as he wanted to cuddle with me.

And that's not normal.

I wanted to make him be just like all the others, but that didn't happen. He was different, and I don't like that he was.

"You should go," I hear Lark say through the crack in the door. I reach for the handle, but can't force myself to turn it.

"I know," he says. His voice is rough and abraded, and I want to go to him and ask where he's going.

"It's better this way," Lark says.

"It is," he mutters.

I hear footsteps and the shuffle of luggage as the front door opens. I press my ear to my bedroom door until I hear the front door close. Then I open my door.

"Oh, Finny." Lark sighs. "What did you do?"

I tug the robe closed around my naked body and step into the hallway. "Did he leave?" I whisper. I don't want Wren to hear me.

"Yes." Lark leans against the wall and tilts her head like she's tired. "He's gone."

My heart trips a beat. "Okay." I force out a nonchalant shrug I don't feel.

"What did you do?"

I look down at the floor. "Nothing." I jerk my eyes up to hers. "He's, like, all the way gone?"

She nods. "Like, took his bags and left."

"Oh." My heart sinks and I don't know why. "Okay."

"You had sex with him?" She stares hard at me.

"Well, yeah…" I probably need to explain–

She rushes to chastise me. "He's not just some random guy."

No. He's not. "I know." I know it the hard way. "He's really gone?" I look toward the front door like he's going to walk back in.

She nods. "Yes. He took Wren's bank book."

"Oh, fuck." I lay my fingertips over my mouth. "Does she know?"

Lark shakes her head. "Not yet." She narrows her eyes at me. "Why him, Finny?"

"Just to see if I could, I think." My voice is so quiet. "Something wasn't right about him."

"He's their brother."

"I know." I lay a hand on my chest. "He's not related to *me*, you know."

She holds up a hand to thwart my objection. "I know that."

"Are you going to tell them I fucked him?"

She heaves out a breath and shakes her head. "What good would that do anybody?"

It wouldn't do anyone any good at all.

But I still can't believe he just took off and left like that.

Tag

Two months later

I hold Julia's hand with one of mine and wipe her brow with a cold wet washcloth. "I hate you!" she screams at me. She's been doing this for about an hour, and I'm pretty used to it by now. "I'm glad I never have to see you again after today."

The delivery nurse shoots me a glance. They know about our crazy situation. But I keep hoping that Julia is going to change her mind, that she'll want to have something to do with our son after today. Our time together is over, but theirs doesn't have to be.

Another contraction wracks her body, and she squeezes my hand so tightly that I wince and pry her fingers away.

"We don't have long now," the nurse says.

Julia relaxes into the bed when the contraction is over and blinks her green eyes at me.

"Can I get you anything?" I ask her.

She shakes her head. "Just be sure they don't lay him on me when he comes out, okay? I don't want to see him."

I brush her sweaty hair back from her face. "Are you sure?"

"I'm sure," she says quietly. "It'll be too hard."

"We can still do this," I say to her. "We can do it together."

She shakes her head. "It's not what I want, Tag. I want him to have the best of everything and I can't give him that."

Neither can I, I think. If not for my sister's money, I wouldn't be able to do anything for him at all.

Julia came to me when she found out she was pregnant. I was over-the-moon excited, but she wasn't. Not at all.

"They can give him everything, Tag," she'd said. *"We can't give him anything."*

"We can do this," I'd told her. *I put my hands together like I was praying. "Please. Just say you'll try."*

"The adoptive family said they'd give me enough money to go to college," she rushed to explain. *"I can get out of here."*

I looked around her dad's tiny little cottage. As the pastor of the church, he was allowed a small house. That was how we'd met. Her dad was counseling me on responsibility.

Julia sniffed. "I want him to have so much more than this. The adoptive family…they want him so bad."

I was away on a mission trip when Julia first found out she was pregnant. She'd sent word to Mexico, but it had taken a few weeks for me to gather enough airfare money to get home. My mission trip wasn't supposed to be over for quite some time, but I'd come home straightaway after hearing the news.

I never should have left in the first place.

"I want him," I said. *I pounded my fist into my chest. "You can't give him away without my permission."*

"I could have just had an abortion and you never would have known," she said quietly.

"But you didn't. And now I do know. And now I want him. You can't give him up for adoption when he has a father who wants him."

She started to cry. "But I have dreams. And they're going to pay for me to go to school. They like me. And they said we can visit him, that we can check up on him." She was pleading with me.

"How much money?"

"You're broke, Tag. Does it matter? Anything they can give him is better than what we can. Can't you see that?"

She was wrong. I could love him. "I want him," I repeated.

"And I want to go to school. I want to be better than…this." She motioned to the room around her. My baby was no bigger than an apple at that point. And she wanted to give him away.

"What if I gave you the same amount of money?" I asked.

She scoffed. "Where would you get that much money?"

My sisters. Jenny and Jessica. They're loaded. "I'll get it."

"Why do you have to make this so difficult?" She heaved a sigh. "Just let him have a good life."

"I will." With me.

Her eyes got big and wide. "You'll sign the papers?"

"No. I'll get you the money."

Her face fell. I hated disappointing her, but I wasn't going to let him go.

"This doesn't feel right," she said.

I crossed the room to stand in front of her and tipped her face up to mine. "None of this feels right. We should be a family."

She stepped back, creating a wide chasm between us. "You left."

"You told me to go!"

"You said you needed it."

"It was for the church," I rushed to say.

"Sometimes I think you love your religion more than you love me."

"I can change," I tried.

She shook her head. "It's too late."

Julia jerks me out of my reverie when she screams and bears down on my fingers. Her belly ripples and moves and the nurse tells me I can look down. I haven't seen any parts of Julia in months, so I don't feel quite right about looking at her vagina, but the draw is too strong. Her legs are parted and I watch him as he slides into the world. The nurse catches him and they lift him to lay him on her belly.

"No," Julia says. She closes her eyes and looks away. A tear runs down her cheek.

"Julia, please," I say. If she sees him just once, she'll change her mind. I'm sure of it.

"Take him away."

He's crying now, and the sound is music to my ears. I walk over to the bassinette where they're cleaning him and look down into his perfect little face. He has my coloring and my hair. "You want to hold him, Dad?" the nurse asks. She looks askance at Julia. But Julia is still staring in the other direction.

"Yes, please," I say. I take him from her and pull him into my chest. "Hello, Benji." He's only minutes old and I'm already in love with him. I can't imagine how Julia could give this up. "Are you sure, Julia?" I ask her.

"I'm sure," she says definitely. She's still refusing to look.

They move us to a different room, one away from Julia. Apparently, it's what they do in adoption situations and that's how they're treating this.

I spend the night with my son in his own room, and I have no idea where Julia is. A nurse comes into the room and says, "The baby's mother would like to see you. She's about to be discharged." I look toward Benji's crib. "I'll watch him. Go ahead," she says gently. She pats my shoulder.

She gives me Julia's room number and I go there. She's dressed in some baggy pants and a loose-fitting top and she has a bag over her shoulder. "Are you leaving?" I ask.

She nods, and a tear slides down her cheek.

"Julia…" I want to hold her, but I don't know if I have the right.

"Don't make it any harder," she says quietly. "Do you have the money?"

I reach into my pocket and take out the cashier's check for forty thousand dollars. I used the rest of the original fifty thousand to buy some baby stuff, and I paid an attorney to take care of the legal stuff so Julia could sign over her rights and I could get custody.

And to finalize the divorce.

"Thank you," she says as she takes the check.

"Are you going to be okay?"

"It would have been easier if he'd gone to a different family," she says. "This way, I'll always know he's with you and that he's not with me, and he'll know it too."

"I'll make sure he knows you love him." My heart is breaking.

She nods. "I did this because I *do* love him. I can't give him anything he needs. And I'm not one hundred percent sure you can either." She looks at me. "Are you going back to your sisters?"

"I doubt they'd have me at this point. I kind of closed that door."

She nods. "Take care of him, okay?" Her voice cracks and I can't stand it anymore. I go to her and pull her into my arms. She falls into me and lets me hold her for a minute, until her sobs quiet.

"When you're ready to see him, call me?"

"I won't."

"You don't know how you'll feel a few years from now."

She nods. "Be good, Tag."

Then I see her new boyfriend standing outside the door. She's leaving with him. She's leaving me with a brand new baby, and she's going to go to college like none of this ever happened. She's going on with her life, and I get to keep the beauty we created together.

I go back to Benji's room and the nurse passes him to me like's a tightly wrapped football.

My phone rings in my pocket and I shift Benji over so I can pull it out. My heart beats faster thinking it might be Julia. Maybe she changed her mind. "Hello?"

"Tag?" a male voice says.

"Yes?"

"This is Josh, and I'm going to marry your sister Star in a few days. We'd love it if you could be here."

"Y-yes," I blurt out quickly. I clear my throat. "*Yes*," I say again. Then my heart falls. "Wait. I don't have any money to get there."

He laughs. "Don't worry, we'll take care of it."

"I'll need a bus ticket."

"When can you leave?"

"Today?"

"I'll take care of the tickets. Give me your full name…"

I give him all the information. "I'll be traveling with my son," I tell him, wincing inwardly.

A pause. "Your *son?*"

"Yes. Is that okay?"

"Hell yeah it's okay," he says on a laugh. "Star will be so happy to see you."

"Is she mad at me?" I ask him. I did just leave with fifty thousand dollars of Wren's money.

"Not that I know of. But she has a vagina, so that might change in about ten minutes," he says with a chuckle.

Something tells me my sister would slap him if she heard him say that. And something else tells me he wouldn't care.

"We'll see you when you get here, man," Josh says.

"Okay," I reply, finally releasing the heavy breath I've been holding.

I shove my phone back into my pocket. It only has a couple of days of service left on it, so I'm glad he caught me now.

I look down at Benji. "We're going to New York, little dude."

We're going to New York to face my family, to face the past, and to run from the future.

Finny

It has been two months since he snuck out like a thief in the night. Two months since he fucked me and then fucked me over. And he had the nerve to show up with a child. I do not like babies, not even babies that are related to two of my favorite people. And particularly not a baby that belongs to him.

Star shoves it into my arms and I hold it out in front of my chest with my arms extended, trying to keep it as far from me as possible while still supporting its head. It squirms, its little feet flailing as it scrunches its face up.

Star lays her head on my shoulder and gazes at it like it's the best thing she has ever seen. She looks at our sister Peck's baby the same way. Star lays a hand on her own pregnant belly and I throw up a little in my mouth. I try to hand it back to its father, but he's talking with Star's new husband Josh and doesn't even notice my struggle with his demon spawn.

"It's going to throw up on me, isn't it?" I ask. I look everywhere but at it. It lets out a wail and its father finally looks over.

Benjamin "Tag" Taggert Jr. has the same scowl on his face as his offspring. He takes the baby from me and pulls it into his chest. "Did the mean little woman refuse to hold you?" he says, baby-talking at it. His eyes meet mine and I look away. He nestles the baby in the crook of his arm and sticks a bottle into its mouth. The kid shuts up immediately. Thank God.

"I didn't refuse," I mumble. I turn and whisper to Star, "Did he just call me *little?*" She rolls her eyes. I have to fight this with humor. If I don't, I'll let my emotions take over and I'll slap his face or kick him in the nuts or do something equally as stupid.

He laughs. "He won't bite you. He doesn't even have teeth yet."

"She doesn't like babies," Wren tosses out. She laughs and her brother rolls his eyes.

"How could you not like babies?" he asks. "They're a gift from God."

I snort. I can't help it. Star gives me a look and I murmur, "Sorry."

I know her brother wants everyone to think he's religious. That he believes in God and blessings and prayer and divine intervention and all that bullshit. But he fucked me senseless and did crazy things to my pussy for quite some time, so I know him for the fraud he is.

Star got married today. Tag showed up out of nowhere with a baby in a carrier, and was here to watch Star get married. Star permitted it. I'm not sure I would have been so generous, considering how he took off two months ago with fifty thousand dollars of Wren's money.

"So, where are you guys staying?" Star asks him.

He glances nervously around. "I'm not sure yet."

"Well, you won't have any trouble finding a hotel, since Wren gave you all that money," I toss out.

He flinches. "Of course," he mumbles.

Alarm bells go off in my head. "Dude, you spent fifty thousand dollars?"

Star heaves a sigh. "Not now, Finny," she says.

"I'll explain everything to you," he rushes to say, speaking directly to Wren and Star. "I promise."

Star smiles at him. "Later."

He nods and looks relieved. "Of course." His eyes meet mine again and I look away, breaking contact.

Star threads her fingers through Josh's and says, "Your baby wants a piece of cake." She bats her lashes at him. She's barely six weeks pregnant, but she's already milking the baby thing.

Josh laughs. "I can take a hint. Anybody else?" He looks around the group. We're all sitting at a table at Star and Josh's reception, taking up space while people mill around us. Star and Josh got tossed in the fountain a few minutes ago, so they had to go and change clothes really quickly. Star came back looking more disheveled than when she left, and Josh had a shit-eating grin on his face.

Somebody got lucky, and it wasn't me.

"I'll take a piece," Wren says. Lark raises her hand, too. She's wearing elbow-length gloves as usual. Pink, to match her dress.

"Me too," I say.

Josh wheels away and Star watches him with longing in her eyes. I pat her on the shoulder. "He'll be right back. I promise." I wrap my hands around my mouth. "With cake!" I whisper-yell.

She laughs.

"You're happy?" Tag suddenly asks her. "Really happy?"

Star nods. "Beyond happy." She has a wistful smile on her face.

"Good."

Star props her elbow on the table and sets her chin in her palm. She nods toward the baby. "Was he what you needed the money for?"

Tag nods. "He was."

"Do you need any more?" she asks.

I choke on my own spit. "Sorry," I gasp out as Wren pounds me on the back.

"No, I took care of everything I needed to take care of. Thank you. I'd offer to pay you back, but I don't have a job yet." His cheeks grow rosy. Is he embarrassed?

Wren shrugs. "It's not like we'll miss it."

He laughs. "Still, I don't want to be a burden."

Then he should seriously think about going home. He's breathing my air. That's a burden all by itself.

"Where's its mother?" I demand.

"I'm…not sure." He looks down at his son. "I wish I knew." He heaves a sigh.

"You'll come home with us tonight," Wren suddenly says. "Star's room is still empty. And so is Peck's. We have plenty of space."

He shakes his head. "I can't take advantage." But hope blooms in his eyes. I can see it. I wonder if he knows that. I wonder if he cares.

He can't *take advantage?* Like running off with fifty thousand dollars while his dick was still wet from being inside me wasn't enough?

"Hello?" I cry. "Perhaps you should ask the other people who live there?" I point to myself. My heart is rattling in my chest like a ping-pong ball in a glass. Lark, Wren, and I share an apartment. I don't think we need more roommates.

Particularly not one who fucked my brains out. Particularly not one who reached deeper inside me than anyone ever has. Particularly not one who scares me.

"He's our brother," Star scolds. "It's not up for discussion."

"Then you should take him home with you."

Star rolls her eyes. "I'm on my honeymoon." She leans close to me and whispers in my ear. "And I'm pretty sure Josh got some sex furniture for me for the honeymoon, and I want to try it out."

"Ewww." I groan. "TMI, Star."

She laughs and looks at Tag. "She'll be nice. I promise." She gives me an evil glare. "*Won't* you, Finny?"

Fuck no, I won't be nice. "No promises." I jerk my thumb toward the baby. "Is he bringing that with him?"

Tag laughs. "I don't go anywhere without him." His gaze locks with mine.

The table goes quiet, because there's force and conviction behind his words.

A man comes up and stops by my shoulder. "Care to dance?" he asks.

I don't know him, but he's handsome and he's got enough balls to ask. I might even fuck him. I've experienced a bit of a dry spell since that night with Tag. It's like my vagina is broken. I look at this guy's face.

Wait. Did I already fuck him? They all blur together after a while. Who knows? "Love to," I say. I get up and follow him onto the dance floor. My night is suddenly looking like it might take a turn for the better.

He pulls me way too close way too quickly. I stiffen and he doesn't take the hint.

"You don't remember me, do you?" he asks, his warm breath moving over my ear.

Now I remember him. I might forget their names and their faces, but I never forget the way they smell. This one smells like body spray and onions.

"I ate you out for about an hour that night," he says. He grins like it's a good thing. Only it wasn't. It lasted for an hour because he was so fucking bad at it.

I grit my teeth. "I remember."

"You didn't return my calls."

I'd told him I didn't want his number and I didn't give him mine. He must have gotten it from someone else.

"I had hoped to hear from you," he goes on to say. He jostles me in his arms like he's hoping to provoke a response.

"I'm not looking for a relationship," I say gently. Then I steel my shoulders and look into his eyes. "And you're not really my type."

He flinches. "I was your type when I was fucking you."

I shake my head. "Not really. You were just there."

He stops swaying to the rhythm of the band. "I was an easy fuck?" His voice pitches on the end of his comment, and people turn to look at us.

It really wasn't that easy, because I had to pretend I liked him while I taught him how to navigate the nether-regions. I don't think he knew what a clit was before that night. "You're welcome," I say flippantly.

He steps back and snorts out a crazy sound. It's not a laugh, and it reminds me of a camel I petted once at the zoo. If he spits at me too...

"Seriously?" he says, his voice getting louder. "You used me?"

"You're welcome?" I say again, but this time I end it in a question.

Hey, I know some guys are happy to get to bag a Zero. This guy apparently is looking for more than one night with the band's bass guitarist.

"You're pretty fucked up. You know that?"

Tell me something I don't know. I grin at him. "Thanks." I like my fucked-up life. I don't particularly need for him to like it too.

"Everything okay?" a deep voice asks from over my shoulder.

I turn and find Tag standing behind me. He must have been dancing with Lark because she's fidgeting right beside him.

"You okay, Finny?" Lark asks.

"How does it feel knowing what a whore she is?" the guy bites out. He smirks. "Or are you just next in line?" he asks Tag.

Tag stiffens, and I think he's going to question me about this guy. But he doesn't. All of his attention is on the douchebag. "Have a little respect, man," he says quietly. I watch his hands as he flexes them, balling and releasing his fists.

"Fuck respect," the douchebag snaps.

Tag adjusts his suit coat. "I'd appreciate it if you'd watch your language. There's no need for profanity."

"Fuck your prof–" He stops talking. Mainly because Tag just punched him on the jaw. His head snaps back and he flinches. It happened so fast that I didn't even see it. I just see his reaction.

"I said watch your language around the ladies." Tag scratches the stubble on his chin.

"Lady? Lady my a–" Again his head snaps back. This time he starts to bleed, his nose dripping blood down over his lips.

Tag reaches into his pocket for a handkerchief and jams it under the man's nose. "You need some help finding the exit?" he asks quietly, leaning toward him.

The douche shakes his head. "No," he mumbles, but it's nasally.

"You should apologize to the lady," Tag says. He steps back so the guy can face me.

I hold up my hands to wave the apology off. "That's really not necess–"

"Yes, it is," Tag bites out. He lifts a brow in the man's direction.

"Sorry," the man murmurs around his handkerchief.

"Sorry for…" Tag waits with an expectant look.

He looks up at Tag with a question in his gaze. He has no idea what he's supposed to be sorry for.

Tag rolls his hand in the air. "Sorry for offending the lady…" He waits expectantly.

"I'm sorry I offended you."

Tag smiles and claps him on the shoulder. "Have a good night," he says.

The man walks away. I see the Reeds meet him at the edge of the dance floor to escort him to the exit. Now I remember how they know him. He's a client of theirs. Oops.

I look up and realize that everyone on the dance floor is watching us. The band starts to play again. Tag holds a hand out to me. "Do me the honor?" he says.

"Close your mouth," Lark whispers fiercely. I clamp my jaw shut. She puts a hand in the center of my back and pushes me toward Tag. I stumble into him and he puts a hand on my hip. He takes my other hand in his and starts to lead me in a dance. Lark goes willingly with someone else to dance.

He bends down to look into my eyes. "You okay?"

"I'm fine." Aside from the fact that I can't breathe. The only man who has ever taken up for me like that is Emilio, my adoptive father. He would go to the ends of the earth, but he's the only man who ever has. "Why did you do that?" I ask.

"Do what?" He looks down at me. It's odd, how much of his attention I have. Almost disconcerting.

"Why did you hit him?"

His broad shoulders shift in a tiny shrug. "He was being rude."

"Because he called me a whore?"

He winces and I know I struck a nerve. "His language was inappropriate. I just helped him realize it."

"So someone referring to me as a whore offends you?" I bite back my grin when I see him flinch again.

"It wasn't necessary to get his point across." He spins me away from him and then brings me back to him. The man has some serious moves, that's for sure.

"Oh."

"You're better than that," he says quietly. "Don't let people speak to you like you're less than you are."

My heart skips. I wasn't enough, apparently, to make him stick around. "What?"

"You're valuable. Worthy. Loveable. Everyone is valuable. Worthy of respect."

I snort. I so do not want to be loveable. I love my family, but I don't love anyone else. I can't. Love makes you vulnerable. It gives people the power to hurt you.

Like him.

"You're pretty darn cute too," he says with a grin.

"Did you seriously just call me cute?" I laugh. I can't help it. "And you said darn."

"Curse words aren't always necessary to get the point across."

"You afraid you're going to go to hell?" I ask on a laugh. Drop a few F-bombs and get the key to the fiery gates.

"I used to be," he says. "Now I'm not so sure."

I realize how stiff he is in my arms. "I'm sorry," I say. "I shouldn't have teased you."

I look up at him. He has dark hair that falls over his forehead in a wave. His eyes are almost black in the waning light, and they're staring directly into mine. I know they're brown, but right now they're dark. And hot.

"I forgive you," he says with a small smile.

"Next time, I'll just tease you about that cow lick." I point up toward his hair.

He chuckles loudly and throws his head back. I watch him, wondering at a man who can laugh with no restraint.

"We need to talk," he says next to my ear. A delicious shiver crawls up my spine.

"No, we don't." I hold tightly to his hand, which is wrapped around mine.

He holds me tighter. "Yes, we do."

"What did you do with the rugrat?" I ask when I suddenly remember his son.

He laughs. "Your mother took him and told me to go and dance. She wouldn't take no for an answer."

"She usually doesn't," I murmur. I look over and find her cuddling the kid while she feeds him a bottle. She winks at me.

"Your family is pretty fabulous."

"Yeah, they are," I agree. My family is *awesome*.

"You're lucky," he says, his voice getting husky. "Not everyone is that lucky."

"You were adopted by an uncle, right?" I vaguely remember the story. The uncle didn't want his sisters, so Tag went there alone.

"Yes." He's stiff as a board now.

"Then you were lucky too."

He doesn't say anything.

"So you're going home with us?" I wince when I realize how that sounded. "I mean," I stumble to say, "I mean you're going to use Star's old room again?"

He nods. "For tonight, at least." He looks down at me. "You don't mind, do you?"

"As long as you promise not to pee on the toilet seat or leave the seat up."

"I'll do my best." He chuckles. "Can you survive my presence for a day or two?"

I shrug. "I'll try. It'll be difficult."

"Thank you for your sacrifice." He laughs again. It's a warm, clean chuckle and my insides melt. He speaks again and it's right by my ear. "I'm sorry if my leaving hurt you. I had to take care of something, and I couldn't explain it at the time. But now I want to tell you about it. Can I?" He waits expectantly.

"Maybe…"

The music stops and he lifts my hand to his lips. He places a tender kiss across the backs of my knuckles, and my belly flips. "Thank you for the dance," he says, his lips lingering over my skin, his breath warm and humid.

"Thank you for punching the douchebag in the face."

"You're welcome." He tangles his fingers in mine and leads me back to my parents. Then he takes Wren to go and dance.

I watch him as he laughs with her, and his cheeks get rosy and I imagine she's teasing him about hitting the guy. But then he looks in my direction and his eyes meet mine. She's teasing him about me if he's searching me out like that. He winks at me, and my heart betrays me with a little flip. What the fuck is that about?

Another man comes up and asks me to dance. I get up and say quietly to him, "Did I fuck you too and just don't remember it?"

He shakes his head. "Not yet," he says with a grin.

I laugh and let him lead me out onto the dance floor. But I can feel Tag's eyes on me and I don't even unbutton the top button of the guy's shirt. I don't run my fingertips beneath his collar. I don't accidentally graze his dick. I do nothing. Because Tag is watching me, and for some reason I feel funny about having him see me put the moves on some random guy. Just in this moment. Just for this second.

The thought irritates me, because I can do whatever I want with my body. It's mine and I don't have to let anyone judge me. Not a single soul.

I'm beyond irritated when the dance is over, because I could have taken this one home with me. Tag is already messing with my game.

I have to fix that. Starting immediately.

Tag

I flex my fist, stretching my fingers because they hurt. I haven't hit anyone in a really long time. I couldn't help it though. He was so rude and inconsiderate. I wanted to shove his teeth down his throat but couldn't, not with her watching. It's bad enough that I hit him.

I would scare her if she actually saw how much turmoil there is deep down in my soul. If she encountered the depth of my rage, she wouldn't look at me the same. None of them would.

I sit down next to Emilio, Finny's adoptive father. He holds his fist up like he wants to pound his fist against mine, like men often do, so I touch mine to his gently. "Nice job," he says quietly.

I don't say anything.

"If you hadn't done it, I was going to."

I look up at him, but still don't speak.

"I'd fight to the death for my daughters." His voice is low and gravelly.

"I'm glad Star and Wren have you." It's true. So glad. I am grateful that they didn't end up where I did. Because where I ended up was so much worse.

"How's your hand?" he asks.

I flex my fingers again. "I'll live."

"Felt good, didn't it?" He watches my face closely.

"Not really. I don't like fighting." I lean forward and balance my elbows on my knees, and let my hands hang down.

His eyes ghost over the shadow of a scar on my upper eyebrow, and then slide across my chin, which is a crisscross of webbing from all the times I landed on my face. "Right," he says quietly.

I watch Fin as she dances. She's graceful and so very beautiful. And so far outside my league.

"You're going home with the girls tonight?" Emilio asks.

I shrug. "They invited me." I look at him, finally, and find him studying me intently. "You don't mind, do you?"

He shakes his head. "My girls are strong women. They can take care of themselves."

My eyes go back to the dance floor and land on Finny again, where she's in the arms of another man. He's looking down at her like he wants to have her for breakfast. Or a midnight snack.

"Don't let Finny's one-night stands bother you," he says.

I jerk my head up. "What?"

He nods toward her. "She brings them home sometimes, but she kicks them out soon after. I don't think she's ever had one stay the night." He shakes his head.

"Does that worry you?"

"Nah," he says. "It would worry me if one ever did stay the night."

"What do you mean?"

Emilio shakes his head. "Doesn't matter."

I wonder if he would feel so nonchalant about it if he knew I was one of her one-night stands and that she didn't exactly kick me out of her bed at the end of the night.

He gets up and goes to get Marta to dance. She puts Benji in his carrier for me. He's sound asleep, but I still start to rock it with my foot.

Emilio whisks Marta out onto the dance floor. She giggles and lets him draw her close.

I wonder to myself what he meant by saying he would worry if she *did* let one stay the night. Strange.

***

Benji wakes me up in the middle of the night four times. I am blurry-eyed and staggering when I smell the coffee start to brew. I lift my head and look around. Coffee? There's coffee?

I toss the covers back and pull on a T-shirt and some jeans. It would probably be prudent to go to the kitchen in clothes. I immediately wonder if Fin will be up and if she'll still be in her jammies. Is it disturbing that I would love to see her in her jammies, looking all rumpled and sleepy-eyed? Probably.

I start toward the kitchen and Wren calls out, "Don't get between Finny and the coffee pot!"

I stop and rub my eyes. "Huh?"

Fin walks toward me, shooting daggers at me with her eyes. I step to the side and let her walk by me. She's wearing loose-fitting pajama pants with the top rolled down, and a thin camisole with skinny straps. And, holy hell, she's not wearing a bra. I look away. My dick is already paying attention. I've never seen her when she first wakes up. Damn, she's pretty.

She stumbles blindly toward the coffee pot and stops in front of it. She fills a mug, and my mouth waters. I want coffee too, but she's taking her own sweet time about filling her cup.

"Don't touch my coffee," she mutters as she shuffles past me, dragging her feet.

I'm already reaching for a mug, but I stop. "What?"

"You heard me," she snaps, but she doesn't look at me.

I put the mug back.

Wren gets up from her spot on the couch and stomps into the room. She takes down a mug and fills it for me, then presses it into my hands.

"Thank you," I murmur. It's all I can do to get the words out. I usually don't speak until I have finished a pot.

"I wouldn't drink that if I were you," Lark says as she comes into the room.

I'm already blowing across the lip of the mug. I look up.

"She'll knife you in your sleep, dude," Lark says. "She's a bitch about her coffee."

"I'll make more," I say. I go to the kitchen table and sit down. There's a newspaper lying there, so I open it and I immediately see a picture of the Zeroes. They're candid wedding shots, obviously taken from a tree or a tall building near the venue.

I stop and read all the articles about Star's wedding, the Reeds, who were in attendance, and all the celebrity gossip about them. Some of it is ludicrous. Other parts are laughable, and even more are just sad. They can't possibly get a lot of privacy.

"Oh, shit," Wren says as she looks over my shoulder at the pictures. She jerks the paper from my hand. "They got pictures of them. Those assholes!"

"I'm just glad no one got a picture of Josh standing at the altar," Lark says.

"He doesn't want anyone to know?" I ask.

They all shake their heads. "That was all for Star. Kind of a private thing," Wren explains.

"Will she be angry about this?"

"Probably not," Lark replies. "I know I'm not going to tell her."

"Why not?" I ask.

The girls all look at one another and grin.

"Because they're busy knocking boots," Finny blurts out. "Bow-chicka-wow-wow."

Heat creeps up my face. "Oh."

Suddenly, Benji cries from the other room. "Can I get him?" Wren asks.

I look down into my half-full cup of coffee. "I can do it." I heave a sigh and start to get up. But Wren is already going toward my room. She goes inside and I hear her cooing at Benji. It makes me smile.

But he's not going to be happy until his tummy is full. I am completely sure of that. I get a bottle from the fridge and stick it in the microwave. I'm still shaking it when Wren comes back into the kitchen carrying him. She takes the bottle from me and goes to sit on the couch, with my son in her arms. He lets her feed him, and looks up at her, his eyes big and wide.

"That's a nice look on you," Finny calls to her.

Wren flips Finny off from over her shoulder.

I laugh.

"Just because you don't like kids doesn't mean they're all bad," Wren says. "This one is kind of cute." She grins down into my son's face.

"It looks better from over here," she sings out.

"He's not an *it*," I say.

She snorts. "Yeah, keep telling yourself that."

"I hope he didn't keep you up last night," I tell her. He only cried for a minute or two each time, but it was still noise when they were trying to sleep.

I came home last night with Lark, and Fin was still dancing with some guy at the party when we left. It shouldn't bother me, and I can't figure out why it does. She's not mine. She never was.

She looks at me and her brow furrows. She doesn't say anything.

The doorbell rings and Lark rolls her eyes. "Ten bucks says that's I-want-to-get-in-her-pants-again flowers."

"Huh?" I get up and go to the door. Fin goes to her room, closing her bedrooom door.

I open the front door, and find a man standing there holding flowers. He looks around the edge of the bouquet and frowns at me.

"What do you want?" I ask.

"I was looking for Finch…" He waits, letting his voice hang there in the air.

"Why do you want her?"

"I brought flowers."

I glower at him and he shrinks back a little. "Why?"

"She's not here right now," Lark calls from behind me.

"Can I leave the flowers?" the man asks.

"Sure," Lark replies. She comes and takes them from him. Then she slams the door in his face.

"That wasn't very nice."

Fin opens her bedroom door and pops her head out. "Is he gone?"

"Yep. You can come out."

"We seriously need to talk to the doorman. They let just about anyone in the building." She glares at me.

They didn't actually let me in that first night. I snuck past them.

She comes back into the kitchen and pours herself another cup of coffee. Then she plucks the card from the clip on the flowers, reads it, rolls her eyes, and tosses it into the trash. "I'll drop them off at the assisted living center. They'll like them." She shrugs and goes to her room. She closes the door.

"She gets lots of flowers," Wren explains. "That particular guy has been bringing flowers every two weeks for the past four months. She takes them to the assisted living center and gives them to the residents who don't have visitors."

So she didn't sleep with this guy recently? The clutch that's squeezing my heart eases a little.

"That's nice, that she takes flowers to the assisted living facility."

Wren snorts. "No one makes the mistake of calling Finny *nice* to her face."

Lark makes an exaggerated gang sign and says, "She's got a rep to protect."

I laugh. Fin's tiny. Like a little Latina fireball. But I don't see her as particularly fearsome.

"You laugh, but she's tough."

The doorbell rings again and I look around. "Should I get it?"

They all roll their eyes but I go to the door anyway. I open it to find a flower deliveryman standing there with a huge vase of roses. There are at least three dozen. How many men did she bring home with her in the past two months?

I take the flowers and put them beside the others.

Fin comes out of her room. She's wearing jeans and a hoodie, and she has her hair pulled back into a haphazard bun.

"Well, shit," she says when she sees the second vase of flowers. "I can't carry that many flowers by myself."

Wren stands up. "Tag can go with you to help." She looks down at my son. "He's asleep."

"Never mind," Fin says. "I'll just make two trips."

"I don't mind," I say quickly.

She looks up at me, her brow quirked. "You sure?"

I want to talk to her anyway. "Yes, I'm sure. Let me get my shoes." I go to my room and slide my feet into my sneakers. Then I dash into the bathroom to brush my teeth. "Are you sure you don't mind watching him?" I ask Wren as I come back out. She barely knows me, after all.

She grins. "As long as you come back," she says.

"I *promise* to come back." I pick up the largest vase of flowers, after I put on my coat. "Ready?" I ask Fin.

"A better question is whether or not *you're* ready," Lark murmurs. "She's only had two cups of coffee."

I guess I'll take my chances.

Finny

My knees tremble as I walk into the place where my mom lives. Part of the reason is because Tag keeps trying to talk to me. "I didn't have any expectations," I say on a sigh.

"I know, but…" His voice trails off.

"Dude, it's all right. I fucked you. I didn't expect you to marry me."

He heaves out a heavy breath and squeezes the bridge of his nose.

I absolutely hate coming to visit my mom, because I never know what I'll find when I'm here. But at the same time I love coming here, because there is a part of me that wishes for more. I want a family. I want to have someone to call mine. But it will probably never be here. Not for any length of time, anyway.

I walk up to the information desk and the receptionist greets me by name. "Finch!" she cries. "So glad to see you!"

"How is she today?" I ask quietly. Tag is standing silently beside me, taking it all in.

"She's not having a great day," the receptionist admits. She winces. "I'm sorry."

I always hope she'll be having a good day. But she rarely does.

"That's okay," I say. "I'll just pop in for a minute." I point to the flowers. "Can you be sure some of the residents who never get flowers get these?"

She smiles. "Of course. I know just who to give them to."

Tag sets his flowers on the counter, too.

"You can go on back home. Thanks for the help," I tell him.

"I'll come with you," he says.

"I don't need a chaperone."

He looks down at me. "I don't want to be your chaperone. But you might need a friend." He falls into step beside me.

"I don't need anything," I mumble.

"Okay," he says. "Then *I* need it." He glares at me.

"You're just a regular goody two shoes, aren't you? Are you going to pray over me next?"

His eyes narrow. "Do you need for me to pray over you?"

"Not on your life," I snap.

He nods. We go through the assisted living facility to the section where mental health patients are housed. The doors are locked and we have to have special escorts to get to this part of the building. If my mother wasn't quite so homicidal, this might not even be necessary.

I stop at her door and look through the tiny window. She's sitting in a chair reading a book. She looks so normal. But she's not. She never has been and she never will be, no matter how much I wish for her to be.

I knock and wait for her to call for me to enter. I have been hit in the head with books, pens, and other miscellaneous stuff since I was a little girl, simply for barging into her room. I've become a little wary.

She calls for me to enter, and I look up at Tag. He stands stoically by the door, but he doesn't try to join me.

"Hi, Mom," I say as I walk into the room. The door snicks closed behind me. Sometimes Mom knows who I am. Sometimes she doesn't. I never know until I get here.

"Hi," she says. Her eyes narrow at me. "What are you doing here?"

I sit down on the edge of her bed. "Just wanted to come by and say hi. To see if you need anything."

"I need some magazines. And some chocolate. And I need for that nurse to stop stealing my toilet paper."

"I'll be sure and get you some chocolate."

"Or did *you* steal my toilet paper?" Her face transforms into a snarl. Suddenly she jumps from the chair and flies at me, her tiny fists flailing.

I grab for her wrists. I have been restraining my mother ever since I can remember. Self-preservation at its finest. She struggles, and she manages to clip me on the mouth. I jerk my head back, but I can already taste the coppery flavor of blood as it floods my tongue.

She turns, picks up a pen from a nearby desk, and comes at me, wielding it like a knife. I freeze. My mother has tried to kill me more times than I can count. This time is no different. I weave to the left and she jabs the pen tip into the soft, meaty part of my upper arm. I wince and try to get my arms around her.

Suddenly, a voice rings out. "Stop!" Tag cries. He crosses the room, his strides quick and even. He wraps his arms around my mother, pinning her hands down. The pen clatters to the floor. She struggles. She cries out. She flails. Her face contorts into a rage-filled, fury-stricken visage of the woman she was a moment ago. "Out!" he shouts at me.

"Don't hurt her," I warn, and I go to get a nurse.

The nurse grabs a vial of medicine from a locked cabinet and runs into the room. She sticks a syringe into my mother's shoulder, and Mom goes limp in Tag's arms. He picks her up and carries her to her bed.

"It might be best if you didn't come by for a few days, Finch," the nurse says. "She's been a little off this week."

"Okay." I try to close the door to the room inside my heart where hope dwells. Hope that she will someday be able to love me.

Mom mutters to herself as she fights sleep.

"Did something happen to set her off?" I ask. Last week, she thought her neighbor stole her purse and she was frantic for days.

"Nothing has to happen, Finch. You know that. And you know it's not your fault. And that it's not you she's attacking, specifically."

I nod. I do know. But it doesn't make it any better.

"We should go," Tag says gently.

I stare down at my mother. She looks old and frail. And soft. And kind. She looks like my mother. Not like some crazed mental patient.

Tag takes my hand in his and gives it a squeeze. I jerk my eyes up to his, and his green eyes meet mine. He appraises me closely. So closely that my skin gets too tight and I try to tug my hand out of his. But he holds me tightly and pulls me toward the door. When it closes behind us, I stop to look through the tiny window and I watch as the nurse bustles around, cleaning and straightening up the mess my mom just made.

I'm still breathing hard. I shouldn't be. I take in a deep breath and blow it out through my lips. I'm ready to leave. So ready. I should have listened when they said she was having a rough day. I shouldn't have tried to visit. It's my own fault she just tried to stab me.

Tag pauses in the hallway and pulls me to a stop beside him. He leans back against the wall, his knees bent so he can look into my eyes a little more deeply. He's much taller than I am. Much, much taller.

He lifts our bound hands in between us and straightens out his fingers. My palm rests along his, and his fingers tangle up with mine. He just holds me like that. I try to pull back, but he doesn't say anything and he doesn't let go.

"Seriously?"

"Shh," he says. "Be quiet for a second. I want to try something."

"You're not going to pray over me, are you?"

"Not right this second. Unless you want me to. And if you do, I will. But no." He breathes in and out slowly, and I realize he's matched his breaths to mine. He looks into my eyes. My breath stops, but he keeps breathing in and out slowly, and I match his pace. "Someone taught me this when I was younger. When my uncle would beat the ever-living crap out of me and I'd get so upset I hyperventilated every time he came into a room."

"I'm not hyperventilating."

"I think I might be, though." He chuckles.

He breathes in and out, staring into my eyes, and I feel myself relaxing. But then he jerks my arm and I fall against him, bracing my hands on his chest to catch myself. "What the fuck was that?" I ask as I push back.

He doesn't let me go, though. He pulls me against him and wraps his arms around me, holding me close. I am stiff as a board, but he's soft and warm and he feels so strong. "Just for a minute," he whispers. "Sixty seconds." He starts to count softly. "One. Two. Three…"

His words are almost as warm as his body. He's holding me tightly, and I let myself melt into him, just for a second. I lay the side of my face over his heart and listen to the steady thump of it, relaxing into him. When he realizes he doesn't have to hold me so tightly, he lifts a hand and drags it up and down my back in soft, gentle sweeps. I burrow in closer to him.

"Thirty. Thirty-one. Thirty-two…"

When he gets to sixty, I'm nearly boneless and I wobble on my unsteady legs like a newborn colt when he sets me back from him. He grabs my elbows and looks down at me. "Okay?"

Well, I was until he held me. Now I just feel…strange. I feel like someone has taken my insides and put them right below the surface of my skin.

"Your mom is mentally ill?" he asks.

I nod.

"Has she always been violent?"

I don't want to answer, but my mouth has decided it has a mind of its own. The traitor. "Yes." Now that it's out there, I rush to explain. "She wasn't always like this. Sometimes she was awesome. She cooked, and played with me, and we went on adventures." I don't know why I feel like he should know all this. Or why I want to tell him. "But then her up days became so much less frequent than her down days." And her lows were really low. "Now she's here, where they can control her meds." And keep her from trying to kill people. Like me.

He starts to walk me down the hallway, but stops in front of a bathroom door. It's the kind with only one room, and he goes inside. He motions for me to follow him.

"What?" I ask.

"Can I check your shoulder?"

"Why?" I look down at my arm. I'm not bleeding.

"Your mother just stabbed you with a pen."

"Oh." I forgot about that in the melee. And the subsequent calm after the storm. I unzip my hoodie and pull the shoulder back.

"She got you pretty good," he says. His fingertips tickle a slow path over my shoulder and I shiver.

"I've had worse."

"I'm sure you have."

I look up at him. He wets a paper towel and wipes away the sticky ooze that has seeped from the small wound.

"It didn't go very deep," he says.

I snort. "That's what she said."

His cheeks redden, but a smile tugs at the corners of his lips. "Why do you do that?" he asks, shaking his head.

"Do what?"

"Deflect with humor when someone tries to care for you."

"Dude, you've known me for half a second," I remind him, my ire rising.

"Tell it to someone who has never been inside you," he says slowly, looking into my eyes.

My heart lurches. "I'm ready to go home."

He reaches past me to throw the damp paper towel away. His arm grazes my boob and he freezes. "Sorry," he says, blushing.

"You totally just did the boob graze. That's, like, the oldest trick in the book."

He laughs. "Yet I've never done it before."

"Liar."

He arches his brow and looks down at me. "I have never grazed a boob that no one asked me to graze."

"So I get to be your first."

Heat creeps up his cheeks again. He's not a virgin. He has a kid, for Christ's sake. Not to mention that he fucked the shit out of me that night.

We walk quietly toward the exit, and a few of the residents call out thanks for the flowers. I wave at them and keep walking.

When we get out on the street, I wince and ask him, "You won't tell my sisters about what happened today, will you?"

He looks confused. "Why don't you want them to know?"

I shrug. "They worry."

"They *should*. She could have hurt you, really hurt you."

I nod. It's not anything I'm not used to.

"Let's make a deal, okay?" He looks at me, his gaze hopeful. "If you'll bring me with you when you come visit, I won't tell anyone."

I roll my eyes. "I told you I don't need a chaperone."

"I don't have to hang out with you," he counters. "I can go visit the other residents. I like talking to people." He shrugs.

"That's all it is? You're not trying to be a macho save-the-damsel bullshit-slinger?"

He puffs out his chest. "Macho, yes. Crap-slinger? Not right this second." He nudges my shoulder with his. "Bring me with you. Please." He puts his hands together like he's praying.

"Fine." But a grin tips the corners of my mouth. "Does this mean we have a date?" I nudge his shoulder this time.

"Do you want it to be a date?"

Do I? Two hours ago, I would have said *fuck no*. But today…after what he did for me with my mom? And after?

"Maybe," I say quietly.

"Then it's a date."

My skin feels too tight and my heart trips a beat. "I'll think about it," I whisper.

Tag

Fin and I get back to the apartment and I find Benji asleep in his portable crib. Wren borrowed it from Peck, who also has a new baby. I didn't have more than a pack of diapers, some formula, and a few pieces of clothing that the nurse passed over in one of those giveaway diaper bags.

And no money to buy anything. I am going to have to find a job. Quickly. But in order to find a job, I'll also have to find someone to care for Benji.

I have to make a lot of plans and figure out what I'm going to do going forward.

I go into the bathroom, turn on the shower, and think.

Benji.

Job.

Money.

Babysitter.

…Finch.

I stop, brace my hands on the counter, and stare at my reflection.

Finch is a problem I didn't anticipate.

Before Finny, I'd only slept with one woman my whole life. There had never been another for me, so it surprised the heck out of me when just looking at Finch took my breath. I can still feel her wrapped around me. Then when I held her at the assisted living facility… The sixty seconds I held her in my arms lasted for the duration of an eye-blink, it seemed.

An eye-blink that rocked my world.

I knew there was something powerful between us. I just didn't realize how powerful. I pulled her against me, hoping just to help her calm down, to center herself. But it was me that went sideways when I held her in my arms.

And now I'm naked in the bathroom getting hard again at the thought of holding her in my arms. We were in a public hallway. She'd just been stabbed by her mother. And I was hard as steel then, and hard as steel now.

Finch is a tiny little thing. Her long dark hair was piled on top of her head in that awkward bun, and I know it hangs down over her shoulders when she sets it free. In my mind, I can still see it spread out over her pillow. I love dragging my fingers through her hair. But since it was pulled up in a bun when I held her, I let myself drag my fingertips up and down the ridges of her spine instead.

I'd halfway expected her to slap me, but I'm not even sure she noticed how she affected me. I'm sure I was just something to do. An easy fuck. Right. I *hope* she didn't notice the way she affected me. She'll think I have bad intentions, and I don't. I don't have any intentions at all.

Or at least I didn't.

Now my only intention is going to be to stay the heck away from Finch Vasquez. Because I feel a connection to her. And connections are scary and dangerous and they make you stupid. I can't afford to be stupid. I have Benji to take care of, and I can't let anything affect the fact that I currently have a roof over his head, some formula to put in his belly, and diapers to cover his behind, but...

...I could lose everything if I'm not careful. And that means I have to be very careful with Finch.

I push the thoughts of her to the side, because she belongs behind a door labeled Happiness, and that door has been firmly locked to me my whole life. I've never been given the key, and I doubt I ever will.

Finny

There's a quick rap on the front door and I jump up to go to my room, but just as quickly the lock turns and the door opens. Peck and Star walk into the room, and they're carrying lots and lots of shopping bags. Peck has a carrier with her baby in it, and Wren immediately goes to get him out of it.

"You t-take Sammy out and he's going to w-wake up hungry," Peck warns.

I look around at all the junk. "Are you doing meals on wheels again?"

Star shakes her head. "We went baby shopping." She grins.

"You're barely pregnant," I scold.

"It's not for me, dummy," Star says. "It's all for Tag and his baby."

I wave my hand over the piles and piles of stuff. "You bought all this for that little thing in there?" I jerk my thumb toward Tag's room.

"Well, Tag didn't have anything with him. We thought he could use some stuff." Star shrugs.

"Wait a minute!" I cry. "Aren't you supposed to be on your honeymoon? Why the fuck are you out shopping instead of screwing that amazingly sexy husband of yours?"

She winces. "Oh my god," she breathes. "My vagina is sore already. I couldn't go one more time on that swing." She grins. "Well, not until tonight, anyway."

"So the swing was a hit?" I ask.

"Oh hell yeah! You can do some crazy shit with that thing. Upside down. Right side up. Backward. Forward. You name it."

Sammy starts to cry, and Peck holds out her arms to take him from Wren. "I w-warned you," she says. Then she sits down and lifts her shirt. He makes a sweet little humming sound as he finds his breakfast. Wren rubs his head. "Be quick about it, dude," she says. "Aunty Wren wants to play with you." He pops off Peck's boob long enough to grin at Wren. Then he turns his head and dives back in.

A noise sounds from Tag's room.

"Oh, another baby! I'll go get that one!" Wren cries.

"There are entirely too many children in this apartment," I grumble.

Wren comes back carrying Benji, and she has the back of her hand pressed against his forehead. "Does he feel warm to you?" she asks. She lowers him like she wants me to take him.

"Oh, hell no," I say.

"Take him. Feel his forehead," she insists.

Begrudgingly, I take him from her and set him in my lap. He looks up at me and immediately starts to cry.

"She makes *me* feel like that too," Star tells him.

"Here, you take it." I hold him out toward Star. She has baby fever, so I assume she'll take him, but she jumps up and starts to sort through bags of baby stuff instead. "Hel-loooo," I cry. Everyone ignores me.

I feel a little wobbly with him in my arms and I'm afraid I'll drop him, so I pull him closer to me. He settles his little head against my shoulder and I look down my nose at him. The weight of him in my arms feels awkward.

"He does feel warm," I say. "You don't think he's getting sick, do you?"

Star unwraps little sleepers and blankets and then takes them to put them in the wash.

"Shouldn't you ask Tag if he *wants* that stuff?" I say.

"It's just some used crap that my neighbor was throwing out." Star grins at me as she comes back into the room. She hides all the empty packages in the trashcan, burying them deep. "And it's not like he doesn't need it. I don't think he has much."

"Except for Wren's fifty thousand dollars," I remind her.

"I used that to get Benji from Julia," a deep voice says from behind me.

I jump, and the baby jumps too. I pat his back to calm him down.

"Who's Julia?" Star asks.

"His mother," Tag answers. He's wearing a pair of jeans and a t-shirt, and he doesn't have shoes or socks on. He rubs a towel across his wet hair, chafing it briskly.

"Where is she?" Star asks.

"I have no idea." He sits down next to me on the couch and smiles at his son. "I didn't think you like babies," he says to me.

"I don't," I grumble. But the baby's being so still and calm. I hold him, because I want to hear the story about the mother of Tag's child.

"Well, babies like you," he says. Then he tweaks the end of my nose with the tip of his finger.

I reach up and cover my nose. I can't believe he just did that. I catch my sisters looking at one another with shocked expressions. "Shut it," I say to them all.

Peck pops her baby off her boob and switches sides, all beneath a blanket that Star handed her from her bag. "So she's not coming b-back?" Peck asks.

He shakes his head. "No."

Star asks softly, "Do you want her to?"

"I did. Even after all that happened, I wanted her to come back. But she'd moved on. It was my own fault, I think."

So you just offered her fifty thousand dollars and she gave you the baby?" I ask.

"No." He scratches his head. "There was a little more to it than that. But to make a long story short, I'm broke and I have Benji." He shrugs. He looks down at Benji, who is starting to fidget in my arms. "Does he look warm to you?"

Benji is still fretful, so Tag gets up and fetches a bottle. I expect him to take the baby from me, but he just warms the bottle and then hands it to me. I look up at him like I'm lost, because I am.

Tag adjusts Benji in my arms so that he's reclining a little, and he sticks the bottle into his mouth. Tag grins at me. "I had to figure it all out too," he says. "I'm still learning."

"I don't particularly want to learn," I grumble.

He laughs. "He likes you," he says quietly.

"Well, that's one of us," I toss back.

I try to maintain my aloofness, but I find that I kind of like the little guy.

Tag's leg is pressed along the length of mine, and my shoulder touches his arm. He could move over some. There's room on the other side of him.

"We brought you some baby stuff," Star tells him. "You didn't look like you had much with you."

He heaves a sigh. "I don't have much. But you really didn't have to do that."

She waves a breezy hand through the air. "Oh, it was nothing. Just some stuff my neighbor was tossing out."

"Liar," he says.

She grins. "Whatever."

They sit and talk quietly while I finish feeding Benji. When his bottle is empty and his eyes are heavy, Tag adjusts him on my shoulder and picks up my hand to show me how to burp him. "Is he going to throw up on me?" I ask, panicking a little.

Peck tosses him a burp cloth and he slides it between my shirt and his kid's face. I relax a little. Then the little guy lets out the biggest burp I ever heard. I'm about to sit him back from me so I can give him some serious props for that massive burp, but before I can move him far enough he spits up on me. White stuff flies out of his mouth and onto my shirt.

"Eww! Take it. Take it *now*."

Tag laughs as he holds out his arms, and I pass Benji over. I get up to go and change. "A little puke won't hurt you!" he calls to my back.

But what worries me more than anything isn't the fact that I just got puked on. It's the fact that I don't mind nearly as much as I should.

Tag

I pace the floor with Benji in my arms. I have no idea what to do with him. He's hot and his cheeks are rosy and he's fretful. I haven't known him that long, but he's never been this fretful before. I bounce him gently on my shoulder and he just cries and cries. He won't take a bottle, and he doesn't need a clean diaper. I already checked.

Wren has been gone all night. I assume she's out with the others, since no one is here but me. I'm all alone, my son is sick, and I have no idea what to do with him.

Suddenly, the front door opens and Fin tumbles into the apartment. She has a man with her, and he has his hand on her ass. She freezes when she sees me. He doesn't. He spins her toward him so he can cover her mouth with his.

Rage clouds the corners of my vision. It's swift and unexpected and I have no idea where it came from. It startles the crap out of me.

The guy who has his hand under her shirt freezes when she covers his hand with hers. "Stop," she hisses. She lifts his hand from beneath her clothes and presses it away. He grimaces and pushes back. She steps away and adjusts her clothing. "Hi," she says quietly to me. "What's wrong?"

I look down at Benji. "I have no idea. He won't stop crying." I look toward her for help, but she's staring at Benji, her brow puckered.

"Who's this, Finch?" the guy asks.

"Shh!" she hisses at him.

He opens his mouth to speak again and she points to the door.

"You may go," she says.

"What?" he croaks.

"*Out*," she says. She walks to the door, holds it open wide, and she makes a quick "move along" motion with her hand. He hangs his head, clenches his jaw, and then squares his shoulders and leaves.

He turns back at the last moment. "Call me?" he says.

She slams the door in his face.

Benji's cries grow even louder. "I don't know what to do," I say.

"Did you take his temperature?"

"I don't have a thermometer."

"Where's his stuff?"

I point toward my room. As I pace back and forth, surely wearing a groove in the carpet, she goes into my room and comes back out with his diaper bag over her shoulder.

"Let's go," she says impatiently. She flaps her hands in the air.

"Where?"

"We're taking the offspring to the hospital, dummy." She motions me forward again. "Move it."

My heart leaps into my throat. "You think he needs to go to the hospital?"

"I have no idea what he needs," she says impatiently. She picks up his carrier and I put him in it.

He doesn't stop screaming. He cries all the way down the hallway and into the elevator, and his sobs turn into sniffles as we get in the cab. He drifts off to sleep, but it only lasts for a moment. Then he cries again.

"I've never felt quite so helpless," I say. I rub the top of his downy little head. He's so beautiful. And I can't even take care of him.

"They'll get him all fixed up at the hospital," she assures me. His car seat is in the middle of the back seat, and she's on one side while I'm on the other.

"They have to see him there even if I don't have money, right?" I ask quietly. My gut lurches. I hate even asking the question because saying it out loud is like affirming all the bad things my uncle told me my whole life.

I would never amount to anything.

No one could trust me.

No one can count on me.

I can't even take care of my son.

I am nothing.

"They'll see him," she says. She lets Benji wrap his tiny little fist around her finger. "One way or the other," she whispers, "they'll see him."

I take a breath and lay my head back against the seat of the cab.

"It's probably nothing," she says quietly.

"You really think so?" I whisper, more to myself than to her.

"Of course." She smiles at me and covers my hand with hers on top of Benji's belly. "Do you know where your sisters are?" She takes out her phone and starts to tap.

"No, I thought they might be with you."

"I left early to come back to the apartment."

Her face colors ever so slightly and she doesn't look at me. She left them to come back to the apartment *with a man*.

"Was that your boyfriend?" I know it's not. But I want to hear about it. It'll take my mind off Benji.

She snorts. "God, no."

"Who was he?"

She shrugs. "Just a guy."

"Just a guy?"

She nods. "Just a guy."

"Your date?"

She shakes her head and heaves a sigh. "Someone I met tonight."

"You brought a guy home you just met?" I blurt out. I hate it as soon as it comes out of my mouth.

"Yes. Don't judge."

"Why?"

She finally looks at me. Her brow furrows. "Why what?"

"Why did you bring home a guy you just met? And why were his hands all over you, if you just met him?"

"Because you spent two months inside my fucking head, Tag. And now you're back and I'm ready to move on. So let me move on, will you?" Her eyes stare into mine and I can feel an electric hum move between us like a live wire.

"Oh," I say. "I see."

"Don't judge," she warns.

I hold up my hands in surrender. "I'm not."

"Yes, you are. Stop it." Her voice is biting and cold all of a sudden.

"I'm not."

"You are."

"No, really–" But in my head, I am. I am. I really am. And I hate that I am. I don't want her to want anyone else. I want her to be mine.

She startles me when she grabs my chin and turns my face toward hers. "I like to have sex, Tag. Get over it."

I bristle.

"It's perfectly all right for a woman to like to fuck men. I like sex. I don't need to defend it, particularly not to you, seeing as how you couldn't resist me either." She lets my face go, but she doesn't stop looking into my eyes. "Don't judge," she says quietly.

"I wasn't judging," I say again. I groan inwardly. I shouldn't say this out loud, but I will. I can't help it. "I'm…jealous." I squeeze my eyes shut tightly.

She startles. "Why?"

I might as well be honest. "It bothers me."

"What bothers you about it?" Her words drip venom and ice.

I choose my words with care. "Because once will never be enough."

The cab stops at the emergency room entrance and I get out, taking Benji's car seat with me. She grabs the base and follows me into the hospital. We go to the desk, and very quickly they have us in triage and then they take Benji from me completely, promising that it'll only be a moment and I'll be with him again.

He's gone, and I'm left with Finny and she's looking at me like I'm going to shatter. And I think I might. But she's also looking at me with a question in her eyes. And I don't know the answer. I know nothing except that I'm scared senseless.

"Come on." She takes my hand and pulls me toward the bathroom. She glances furtively left and right and then pulls me inside. "Sixty seconds," she says.

She opens her arms to me and I don't even think before I pull her against me. I need this. I need her. I need for someone to take away the helpless feeling I have.

This time when I hold her, my dick doesn't get hard. But I do use her. I use her warmth and her softness and I listen to her sweet voice as she counts to sixty. It's over too soon. She steps back from me and I'm at a loss.

"Let's go wait for Benji," she says. She threads her fingers through mine.

"I wasn't judging," I say quietly as we sit side by side in the waiting area.

She sighs. "Okay."

"I really wasn't. I was thinking that I can understand why you get so many flowers."

Her brow puckers. "What?"

"Because you're pretty awesome," I say quietly. "If you were all the way mine, I wouldn't want to give you up either."

She strokes a hand up her arm when goose flesh erupts. "I don't do relationships."

"I don't do one-nighters."

"Then it's a good thing we're really good friends, isn't it?" she says.

The nurse comes out and calls my name. We get up and walk to her. "Are you the mother?" she asks Fin.

Fin starts to shake her head but I say, "Yes." I don't want to go back there alone. Not right now. I want her with me to soften the blow of whatever is wrong with Benji. I can't lose Benji. And I need Fin to help make it all right.

I want to explore why sixty seconds holding Fin was better than a single moment I ever spent with Julia, but I can't do it right now. Now I have to find out what's wrong with my son. When he's better, I'll deal with the rest.

Finny

He looks absolutely helpless. Tag, I mean. Not Benji. Benji actually looks comfortable. He's not crying right this second. They hooked him up to IVs and gave him some medicine to bring down his fever. It was just an infection. A simple one. Antibiotics should clear it up. They did a bunch of blood work and pronounced him okay.

Tag is a little bit more of a problem.

"Would you stop pacing?" I say.

"I'm not pacing," he argues. But he doesn't stop walking.

"Okay, then stop walking briskly back and forth. You're causing a draft."

He stops and stares down into the bassinette. "In my head, I'm trying to plan," he says quietly.

"Plan for what?"

He shrugs. "Plan for his life. Plan to take care of him. Plan to be a good father who can fulfill his needs. I don't even have a job, Finny." He heaves a sigh and then scrubs the heels of his hands into his eyes.

"It's late," I say. "You can think about all that tomorrow."

"I have to find a job."

"Tomorrow."

"And someone to watch him while I work."

"Dude, you have two sisters and they have three sisters and a mother. I think you'll be covered."

He snorts. "I can't ask my family to watch him. I can't keep taking advantage." He grips the edge of the bassinette so tightly that his knuckles turn white. "Don't you see?" he bites out. "What if I caused this?"

"What do you mean?"

He stands there with his eyes closed tightly. "I was angry when I came back from my mission trip and found out Julia didn't want to be with me anymore. I did some things I regret. Said some things I regret."

"To her?" She probably deserved it.

"To God," he says. "I said it to God."

Oh. Now I get it. "And you think God's mad and he's punishing you?"

"I think I wasn't grateful for the gifts I've been given, yes."

"Bullshit."

His head jerks up. "What?"

"Bullshit," I say again. I hold up my hands when he starts to speak. "Oh, wait, I cursed. You think something terrible is going to happen to me?"

"That's not amusing."

"When I'm trying to make you laugh, you'll know it."

"I'm just worried that my doubts could cause a ripple effect," he says quietly.

"You still have faith, right?" I don't fully understand faith. Not now. But I respect the fact that he has it.

He nods. "Of course." He winces. "But I was angry. And I said some things I shouldn't have."

"So, unsay them," I tell him with a shrug.

He looks confused. "What?"

"God's not a vengeful dude, dumbass. He's benevolent. He's all-knowing, too, so he knows your heart. Unsay whatever it is you said and you can be done with it."

"You believe in God?" he asks me. He stares into my eyes.

I drag my finger up and down a crack in the wall. "I used to spend a lot of time with the preacher and his wife in our small town. When my mom would go off the deep end, they took me home with them. So, yes, I know who God is."

"Will you think I'm stupid if I believe?" He watches my face closely.

"Dude, I already think you're stupid."

He grins. "When everything else was taken from me, my faith sustained me. If I abandon it, I feel like I'll be abandoning a part of myself."

I shrug. "So don't." My phone chimes and I look down at it. "Your sisters are on the way." I get up from where I'm sitting. "I should probably go."

"Don't," he says quickly.

"What?"

"Don't go. Please." He tilts his head and smiles at me. "*Please*," he says again.

My heart jolts. "Why do you want me to stay?" I hold my breath.

He shrugs. "I like you."

"You *like* me? What are you, twelve? So what's next, I get to ride on the handlebars of your bike?"

He smiles. "Would that be so bad?"

No. No, it wouldn't be so bad. It would be kind of awesome. "We already have a date planned, and it involves visiting the inmate at the asylum," I remind him. I don't want him to think of me as a normal girl. I want him to remember I'm *not* a normal girl and I never will be.

"Something to look forward to," he says with a grin.

"I don't kiss on the first date, just so you know," I say. I wince as soon as it comes out of my mouth. I shouldn't have said that.

"Oh, you'd kiss me," he says with confidence.

My heart skips. "You think so?"

"Yep. I got mad skills."

Benji starts to fret in his crib, so I get up and go to him. I lay my hand on his belly and he stares up at me, calming immediately. His big eyes blink at me as he flails his hands and feet. "You feel better, Benji?" I ask him. He kicks again.

Tag walks up behind me, and I can feel him from the back of my head all the way to my shins. He puts a hand on my hip and sets his chin on top of my head, staring down into the bassinette. "I was so worried," he says. "I'm so glad you came home when you did."

My gut wrenches when I think about who I arrived home with and what I was about to do. "Me too," I agree. I'm not ashamed. Not by a long shot. But I wonder what it might be like to have a family of my own and one man to come home to. I shake the thought aside. I lay my hand over his. "That guy…" I squeeze my eyes shut tightly and hold my breath, trying to settle my insides. "I just met him. There hasn't been anyone else for me since…that night." I look up at him. "Nobody."

He smiles. "Okay." He kisses my cheek, lingering ever so briefly.

I want him to tell me that there was no one else for him too, but I don't feel like I have a right to ask.

"Guess what?" he whispers.

"What?" I whisper back.

"There hasn't been anyone else for me either." He kisses the tip of my nose.

My belly flips. "Not even when you went back to see Julia?"

He shakes his head. "Our relationship was over before I ever came here the first time." He smiles a quirky grin at me. "And I had this tiny little brunette on my mind the whole time I was gone."

My heart warms.

"So, when are we going on our date?" he asks. He brushes my hair to the side so that it doesn't tickle his face. His warm breath brushes my neck and goose bumps erupt on my arms. My nipples go hard and I'm suddenly really glad he's behind me so he can't see it.

"Whenever I get more flowers," I say with a laugh I don't feel. There's no humor in it at all. None.

He stiffens behind me. "Okay," he says.

The door to the room we're in suddenly opens and Wren and Star walk into it. They stop in the doorway and freeze when they see him standing behind me with his chin on my shoulder. I bump him so he'll step back. He does, and I feel the loss of him right away.

"Everything okay in here?" Star asks. Her eyes skitter from him to me and back.

"Benji's better," I chirp. I stare into the crib. "It was just an infection."

Star smiles. "Oh, thank goodness." She walks over to the bassinette and looks into it. Suddenly, she covers her mouth. "I think I'm about to throw up," she says, and she races from the room.

"I'll go and make sure she's all right," Tag says, and follows her out.

Wren stares at me for a beat too long, her eyes full of censure. "What the fuck are you doing, Finny?"

I point into the crib. "He was sick," I say. "I was just trying to help."

"That's not what I mean and you know it." She jerks a thumb toward the doorway. "You were all but snuggling with my brother just now."

"I was not," I protest. But I kind of was. And I liked it. I don't like that I liked it, though. I blow out a heavy sound of protest through my lips.

She narrows her eyes at me. "I don't think he's emotionally available, Finny," she says quietly.

"Good, because I don't have emotions."

She snorts. "Tell that to someone who doesn't know you, bitch." She stares at me. "I always wondered what kind of man it would take to get to you."

I scoff. "He hasn't gotten to me, hooch."

"Oh, he has *totally* gotten to you."

I can't tell if she's joking or not. "What makes you say that?"

"You let him hold you, Finny. You never let anyone hold you." Her voice gets soft. "Why did you let him hold you if you don't like him?"

"He didn't exactly ask!" I blurt out. I point to the kid. "We were just looking at Benji!"

Her voice goes softer. "He wasn't looking at Benji, Fin. He was looking at you."

I snort. "He was not."

"You can lie to yourself. But you can't lie to me."

I say nothing, because there's nothing to say.

"Thank you for taking care of him tonight," she says. "I don't think he has had anyone to take care of him in a long time."

"I didn't do anything."

The door opens, and Tag and Star come back into the room. Wren stops her yammering, thank God. "You okay?" I ask Star.

She nods. "Just had to toss my cookies." She lays a hand on her belly. "Being pregnant is sickening." She looks at Tag. "Was Julia sick a lot?"

He shrugs. "I don't know," he says quietly. "I wasn't there."

"Well," I say, "since everything here is under control, I'm going home."

Tag's brow furrows. "Is that guy waiting for you?"

"What guy?" Wren asks. She looks from him to me and back.

"Nobody waits for me," I quip and force out a laugh. "See you guys later." I go out the door, and stop to take a breath.

The door opens behind me and Tag runs smack into me. "Sorry," he says. "I was trying to catch you." He holds me steady by my elbows.

"Did you need something?"

"I just wanted to tell you…"

I stuff one hand into the pocket of my hoodie. "What?"

"I would totally wait for you," he says quietly.

I pick at the peeling paint on the wall with my fingernail. "You're already waiting for your baby mama," I say, trying to sound flippant.

He shakes his head. "No."

"Why not?"

He looks toward the doorway to his son's room. "She's not who I thought she was." I must look blankly at him because he goes on to say, "She left him. The woman I loved would never have done that."

"Maybe she had a reason."

"She didn't pick me. That's all I know." A muscle in his jaw jerks. He takes a breath and relaxes a little. "When I get myself settled, I'm going to ask you out on a real date."

My heart jumps. "Will that involve sticking two straws in a soda? Or will you let me wear your class ring?"

He smiles. "You'll have to wait and see."

He bends down and kisses my cheek, his warmth hovering delicately over my skin like the sweetest of breaths, and then he waves at me and goes back to his son. I sink back against the wall, because my knees are suddenly weak.

I don't like this feeling. I don't like it at all.

Tag

I walk back into the room and find both my sisters with their arms crossed in front of them, glaring at me. I stumble to a stop. "What? Did I do something wrong?"

"What's up with you and Finny?" Wren asks. She's still scowling.

"Nothing. Why?" I cross the room and pretend to be busy looking down at my son.

"Finny doesn't let anyone *hold* her," Wren says vehemently.

"I wasn't *holding* her," I toss back. "I was just standing behind her." Actually, I was sniffing her perfume like a total perv, but I'm not going to tell them that.

"Standing behind her *holding* her," Star clarifies. "Did you slip her some kind of drug or something?"

"No! I don't have to slip a girl a drug to get her to like me."

"Fin doesn't like anyone," Wren tells me.

"Tell that to the guy she brought home tonight. She was liking *him* all over the place." I blow them off.

"No," Star says slowly, "she was going to have sex with him."

I look up. "What's the difference?"

Wren laughs. "Oh, you're in major big trouble."

Star joins her in her merriment. "You have no idea," she says.

They're starting to get on my nerves. "Explain, please."

"Finny grew up different from the way we did," Star says.

"Everyone grows up differently." I can't tell where she's going with this.

Wren holds up a hand. "No, you don't understand. She grew up *very* differently." She points from me to Star and back to herself. "We had parents who loved us until they were gone. Finny never had that. Not really. So she has a hard time getting close to people."

"I already met her mom," I say quietly.

"*What?*" Star reaches out to grab a nearby chair like she's going to fall over. "You met her mom?" She starts to grin and she looks at Wren. "He met her mom."

"It was an accident, really," I say.

"What happened when you met her mom?"

Well, I had to subdue her to keep her from killing Fin, and then let someone jab medicine in her so she would pass out. But I can't betray her confidence. I lie. "It was just a normal meeting."

"And how was she when you were there?"

"Who?" I ask, trying to sound stupid so they'll drop it.

"Finny's mom. How was she?"

Homicidal. "Mom-like."

"Mm-hmm." Star nods. "You're lying."

"Am not."

"Are too."

"Am not!" I say a little louder.

"Whatever," Star says. She walks over to the bassinette. "Can I hold him?"

"If it'll make you stop grilling me, yes."

Careful of the IV, she picks Benji up and sits down in a rocking chair with him. She holds him close. She stares down at him for a few minutes of blissful silence. Then she finally looks up. "I'm really glad you're here," she finally tells me.

I nod. "Me too."

"We're going on tour in two weeks," she says. "Just six small-town gigs."

"Okay…"

"We want you to go with us. We need some help with set-up and tear-down."

"Okay," I say again.

"It pays."

"I don't need for it to pay. You're already putting a roof over our heads."

"And Paul Reed says he needs some help at his apartment building. Some kind of maintenance job. You interested?"

"Heck yeah, I'm interested. But what do I do with Benji?"

"When we're on tour, Marta can watch him. She goes with us sometimes. She's going to be watching Peck's baby too, so one more won't matter."

Anyone who says one more baby won't matter has never had a kid around. "Are you sure?"

She nods. "I already talked to her about it. And when you're working for the Reeds, we'll take turns watching him."

"Seriously?" The band that was so tight around my heart eases a little.

Star smiles at me. "Seriously." She looks down at my son and then back up at me. "That's what family is for. To pick us up when we fall."

"Or when we get knocked down," Wren says. She stares at me hard.

"Thanks," I say quietly. "I'll get myself sorted out and pay you back, I promise."

Star shakes her head like I'm a child caught being naughty. "We know where you live, Tag."

A grin tips the corners of my lips.

"So, are you going to ask Finny out on a date?" Wren asks.

"You think she'd say yes?" I wait with bated breath.

Star snorts. "Hell no."

My heart falls.

"She's going to say no. She's going to say she doesn't date. She's going to tell you to go fuck yourself. And she might even try to kick you in the nuts."

I cover my package and wince just thinking about it. "Maybe I won't ask her…"

Star grins. "You won't be able to avoid it. She's magnetic."

Wren's voice is quiet when she says, "Nobody deserves a happily-ever-after more than she does."

"Thanks for the advice," I say. My mind is already whirring with all the ways I can get Fin to like me. And all the ways I might screw it up so she kicks me in the nuts.

The latter is much more likely.

Finny

Tag and his offspring have been here for two weeks. Two weeks of a baby crying in the night. Two weeks of overflowing trash cans and a fridge full of formula bottles. Two weeks of cuteness overload.

Okay, I admit it. The kid *is* cute. And Tag is pretty damn cute, too. He's good and kind and he's an attentive father, or at least he's trying to be.

I hug my pillow to me tighter and pound my fist into it. The kid has been crying for a couple of minutes and Tag hasn't picked him up.

I get up and walk into the kitchen. The sound gets louder.

I walk to his room and fling open the door. "Can you shut that thing up?"

I freeze when I see that the bedside light is on but Tag isn't in the room. Where is he? Then I hear the shower running. Tag worked late, working for the Reeds. I heard him when he came in, and I heard him tell Wren good night. He must have gone straight to jump in the shower after.

I walk to the side of the crib and look down. Benji's face is all red and he's kicking his arms and feet. I lay my hand on his belly and he kicks harder, but he doesn't stop crying. I scoop him up in my arms and cradle him tightly. Wren says babies like to be cuddled. This one doesn't, because he just screams even louder.

I walk to the kitchen and get one of his bottles from the fridge. I warm it up really quickly, and he roots around as I stick it in his mouth, and finally latches on to it. Okay. This is kind of cool. I can feed him and then I can lay him back down.

The house is completely silent, aside from his sucking-humming noises and the sound of the fan running in the bathroom. I hear the door open, and Tag walks into the room. He skids to a stop and I have to remind myself to breathe.

He's wearing a towel. And that's all. The corner of the towel is knotted in his fist. His long legs are bare except for a tattoo on his lower leg, and his chest is completely exposed. Water drips from his wet hair across his chest, and I have a crazy impulse to lick it away.

Holy shit. This is bad. I look down at Benji and watch him as he greedily devours his bottle. "He was crying," I explain.

"Did he wake you?" He runs a spare towel across his hair.

I shake my head. "I was awake."

"I didn't realize you were here," he says.

"Apparently." I finally look up at him and I let my eyes wander over his torso.

His face colors and he turns toward his room. "I should put some clothes on," he says, his voice gruff.

"Not a bad idea," I whisper.

He closes his bedroom door behind him, and comes back out a minute later. He's wearing a t-shirt and some pajama pants. His feet are bare. "Do you want me to take him?" he asks. He reaches like he's going to take Benji out of my arms. I block him by turning slightly away.

"He's almost asleep." I look down into his perfect little face. His mouth is slack around the bottle and I jiggle it between his lips to get him to suck. He grabs hold again and starts to drink.

"You're pretty good at that," he says quietly.

"Necessity is the mother of intention," I quip.

He grins. "Isn't it invention?"

"I know." I smile back at him. "It's something my dad used to do with me. He'd toss out these mis-worded quotes and sayings. He got us all doing it."

"Your real dad?"

I nod my head. "Emilio."

Tag looks at me quizzically.

I shrug. "He's the only dad I've ever had."

Tag nods.

"I'm going to go and visit my mom tomorrow," I say quietly.

He rubs his hands together quickly. "Oh, a date! What time?"

"Whenever I get up."

The bottle falls out of Benji's mouth and I set it to the side. He's sound asleep.

"Is he supposed to burp or something?" I ask.

He shrugs. "Sometimes he does. Sometimes he doesn't." He holds out his arms and I settle Benji in them. I run my hand across his hair, and I feel a sudden and overwhelming urge to bend and kiss his fat little cheek. So I do.

I lean over and hover over his baby-scented hair, breathing him in, with my eyes closed. Then I press my lips to his forehead and hold them there.

When I look up, I find Tag staring at me. Suddenly he grabs my shirt and jerks me toward him. His lips hover over mine. "Tell me not to kiss you," he whispers, his eyes skittering across my face.

"Don't kiss me," I say.

His lips land on mine, hard. There's nothing soft or sweet about his kiss. It's hard and hot and I kiss him back. He sucks on my lower lip, and I nibble at his. I kiss him until some of the passion fades and I'm left with warmth and want.

"I shouldn't have done that," Tag whispers, his face close to mine.

I nod. "Bad idea." I swallow so loudly I can hear it.

He tips my chin up so I have to look at him. My eyes refuse to rise and I look everywhere else. "It has been hell having you around for two weeks and not being able to touch you," he tells me.

Finally I look at him. "What's stopping you from touching me?"

"I want to wait. Until it's right."

He leans and presses his lips to my forehead, lingering there just like I did with Benji. I feel the warm rush of air from his nose as he drinks me in, just like I did with his son. Only it's not fondness or kindness I'm feeling from him. It's heat.

"I should go to bed," I say.

"Yeah, you should."

"Good night," I whisper.

"Night," he replies.

Instead of going to my room, I go to Lark's. I open her door and slip inside. She's lying in her bed listening to music with her headphones on. I fall onto the bed next to her and finally let out a breath.

She tugs her headphones from her ears and stares at me. "Have you been drinking?"

"No." But I feel like I have.

She lifts her hand to my forehead. "No fever," she says.

"Nope." I look at her, and a grin breaks across my face.

"Oh, my god," she exclaims as she sits up. "Did you meet someone?"

I've met so many someones that I can't keep up with them all. "Sort of." I wince.

Her eyes narrow. "What do you mean, sort of?"

"Tag sorta kinda just kissed me a little bit," I blurt out. It rushes out of my mouth like wind through a tunnel.

"What!" she screeches. I cover her mouth with my hand.

"Shh!" I hiss. "He'll hear you."

She grins and starts to whisper. "So, how was it?"

"Perfect," I say. My heart does a little dance in my chest.

"Oh, Finny…" She looks upset all of a sudden.

"What?"

"I was wondering how long it would take."

My heart trips again. "What do you mean?"

"I saw him sneaking out of your room that night, Finny," she says quietly.

"Oh." Forgot about that.

"And I haven't seen you bring anyone else home since then."

"Yeah," I breathe, wincing, "I better get on that."

"You like him."

"No…" I draw out the word.

"Yes, you do."

I bury my face in my hands. I groan. "I don't know." I look at her finally. "Tell me what I should do."

She lies back beside me and we both stare up at the ceiling. She takes my hand and holds it and doesn't say anything more. The soft texture of the gloves she always wears slips across my skin.

Her breaths go soft and even and I realize she's asleep. I get out of her bed and steel my shoulders. I'm going to tell Tag that I can't do this. I can't be that girl.

I go to his room and lift my knuckles to knock.

"Don't do it," a voice says through the crack in the door.

I freeze. "Don't do what?"

"Don't knock on my door."

"Why not?"

"It's a bad idea."

"Okay." I turn to go back to my own room.

The door opens and he sticks his head out. "I've been waiting for you to come and knock on my door so you can slap me for that kiss."

"I wasn't going to slap you."

"I know." He lays his forehead against the doorjamb of his room. "That's what scares me."

I nod, although I don't understand at all. Not a bit. "Okay."

I go to my room and he closes the door to his. I look back at his closed door for a moment.

What the fuck was that?

Finny

Music pounds in my veins like a heartbeat. It's quick and consuming and I'm so damn hot that I'm turning myself on, and all I'm doing is dancing.

My personal security guard is standing over by the bar, pretending to nurse on a Jack and Coke, but I know it's just diet soda. I don't always need a security guard, but when I go out in a crowd and I'm alone, it's best to have someone to help if things go bad. Jason's gaze wanders around the room, and he scowls when he sees the guy I'm dancing with get a little too close. He starts to get up, but I shake my head at him. He narrows his eyes at me in a silent question.

No, I don't need for you to come and pull him off me. This is not the one I want. The one I want smells like baby spit-up and talcum powder.

"You want to go to my place?" the guy asks, his mouth close to my ear.

I shake my head. "I just want to dance!"

Before Tag, I would have said yes to him. I would go and not think twice about it. I might come twice. Maybe more if he's any good, but I wouldn't even have to think about it. Yes, I might orgasm. But something tells me I would still feel empty inside after I get home. I'd shower off the scent and the feel of sex, and then I'd wrap my arms around my pillow and fall asleep.

The live band stops playing and we all clap.

"We're taking a five minute break," someone says quietly into the mic.

"Thanks for the dance," I say over my shoulder. The guy clutches his chest like I've stabbed him, but I walk away. I start toward the bar so that I can get something cool to drink.

Jason, my personal bodyguard, pretends like he doesn't know me, so I lean into his side. "So, are you ever going to fuck me or what?" I smile and bat my lashes at him.

He grins a sideways kind of smile. "I don't think my wife would appreciate it, Fin, but thank you for thinking of me." He rolls his eyes and sticks his tongue out at me. Jason is pushing fifty, and he has been happily married for twenty-five of those years. He mumbles something about jailbait as a scantily clad young woman walks by us.

"How's Norma?" I ask.

"She's pissed at me. Apparently, I was supposed to have been a mind reader or some shit."

I bump his shoulder with mine. "What did you neglect to do?"

He pretends to look offended. "What makes you think it was *me?*"

I look down toward his lap. "Because you have testicles, dude."

He pushes his knees together. "Stop talking about my man parts."

"I didn't say I want to lick them or anything, Jason," I say with a grin.

He looks down his nose at me. "Do you kiss your mother with that mouth?"

I freeze. He realizes his mistake immediately, because he reaches to grab me when I pull away.

"I'm sorry, Finny. I didn't mean it." He pushes me back onto the barstool. "I meant Marta."

"Yes, I do kiss my mother with this mouth," I toss back. I wave my finger around the room. "And I kiss other people, too. Some people happen to like my advances." I glare at him. I like to mess with him but, truth be told, he's like a comfortable old uncle. He's been on my detail long enough that he feels like family.

"When you going to settle down, Finny?"

"Never," I tell him, and I suck down the last of my water.

Someone taps the mic at the front of the room, then clears his throat. I look over at the stage. "I just heard a rumor that someone famous is here," the club owner says. He shades his hand with his eyes and starts scanning the area.

Oh, shit. Jason grabs my arm and gets ready to pull me toward the back exit.

"Wait," I say. I hold up one finger. He doesn't let me go.

"You're going to get both of us killed," he murmurs at me. "And Norma will chop my balls off if I let you get hurt." But he stands still and lets me see what they want.

"One of the members of Fallen from Zero is here. Their lead guitarist. Finch Vasquez," he says, searching the crowd. Then he places his palms together like he's praying. "Finny, the last time you were here, you graced us with a song." He holds up a guitar. "Will you do us the honor?"

"What do you think?" I mumble at Jason.

"I think you're stuck now," he mumbles back. He walks beside me, presiding over me like I'm the most important person on the planet. Someone reaches out to touch my shirt, and he brushes the arm away.

I walk up to the stage and take the guitar. I hold the mic away from me. "Just one song," I tell him.

The club owner grins and nods. "Just one." He leans over and kisses my cheek.

"I have one condition," I say into the mic. I reach over and take a hat off a guy's head in the crowd. "If you want me to play, you guys have to fill up the hat. I'll give the money to the homeless shelter on the way home. Deal?"

I wait to hear their enthusiastic responses. The hat starts to move around the room, and people drop cash into it. I see Jason clear it out and stuff the money in his pocket, and then start it moving again.

I settle on the edge of a stool and balance the guitar on my lap. I pluck at it.

"I can't believe Finny Vasquez is playing my fucking guitar!" the owner of the instrument crows.

I grin and start to play. I have a new song I just wrote, so I might as well try it out, right? I suddenly clap my hands over the strings and stop.

"My sister Peck just had a baby boy two months ago," I say into the mic. "This one is for her."

I start to play again.

Sometimes when I see my sister with her baby boy, I watch them together. Her eyes fill with so much love and joy that it makes me ache. I never had that. Not for a moment. Not until I met Marta did I know the definition of unconditional love.

In the first minute,
I wondered how you could be so perfect.
In the second minute,
I wondered how you could be so small.
In the third minute,
I wondered how you could be so fragile.
In the fourth minute,
I wondered how you could be so bald.
In the fifth minute,
I watched you breathe.
In the sixth minute,
I watched you cry.
In the seventh minute,
I watched you stretch.
In the eighth minute,
I watched you love.

You were born knowing
That you were loved.
You were born knowing
That you were adored.
You were born knowing

That you would be cared for.

And in that moment,

Her dreams came true,

Because she was loved by you.

I repeat the beginning and the chorus a couple of times, and by the time I'm done, I've upset myself a little, because *I* wasn't born knowing I was loved. In fact, it was just the opposite. I was born knowing I was hated.

You were born knowing

That were you loved.

You were born knowing

That you were adored.

You were born knowing

That you would be cared for.

And in that moment,

Her dreams came true,

Because…she…was loved by…you.

My voice goes quiet and I wait. The audience blinks at me and then they start to clap. A few women at the front wipe their eyes and someone else proposes marriage.

I pull a felt-tip pen out of my pocket and hold it over the guitar, silently asking the owner with my eyes if he'd like for me to sign it. He pumps his fist and shouts, "Hell yes!" So I sign it with a flourish. I stuff my Sharpie back in my jeans pocket and hand him his guitar.

He tries to hug me, but Jason gets between us. The guitar owner holds up his hands like he's surrendering to the cops.

Jason leads me off the stage and we walk back to the bar, I can't stay here now that everyone knows who I am. I'm aware of it, and so is Jason. He's hyper-aware of it, if the way he's clutching my arm is any indication. "We need to get out of here," he says.

And that is when things go ridiculously bad.

Tag

I stand with my foot against the wall and cross my arms in front of my chest. God, she's beautiful. Music comes out of her mouth and straight from her fingertips into the guitar and it's like it's shooting directly from her soul into mine.

She sings of babies. And babies should be laughter and light and goodness, but what I don't think most people realize is that she's singing about loss. She's singing about her own life, and all the things she missed.

My gut clenches at the look on her face.

I left my own son at home with my sister Wren. He's only a few days old, but Wren wanted to sit and hold him, so she asked me to come and check on Fin at the bar. Honestly, I smell a set-up, but it's a trap I'd give just about anything to fall into.

Finny signs the guitar with a flourish, and I wait for her to clear the stage.

I see the crowd of people surround them, and I watch Jason as he tries to get between them and her. But he's only one man.

I guess when you're a famous rock star this happens, but I never expected it to happen quite so fast. I push my way into the crowd, and Jason sees me and yells, "Get on her other side!"

I nod and shove through the throng. Finny curses as someone grabs the arm of her shirt and rips. I see the flash of her pink bra as the seams render, and my vision goes hazy with rage.

I spin the guy who just tried to strip her down to face me and punch him in the throat. He goes down like a stone, so I step over him and go for another. I take a sudden punch to my own jaw that makes my teeth snap together, and then I see that it's a woman. I can't hit a woman.

The club owner and his security are trying to help too, and they push the rest of the crowd back. Fin is on the floor, and I realize that I'm lying on top of her.

"Umm," she says, "Tag…"

"What?" I can barely get my breath, much less speak.

"You're kind of squishing me."

I lift myself up on my elbows and look down at her face. "Sorry."

Then I realize how we're lying. Her legs are spread, and I'm resting between them.

"Shit," I say. "Sorry." I scramble to get off of her.

She laughs and pulls me back down. "I kind of liked it," she says with a giggle.

Heat creeps up my face as my dick gets hard. Crap. Didn't mean for that to happen.

"Well, you *do* like me," she says close to my ear. She laughs. "I thought you were immune to me by now."

I'll never be immune to this woman. "Stop it."

She laughs. "I'm not the one pressing his dick into my soft parts, Tag," she says.

This time, I do scramble to get up. Her eyes linger on my dick. "Impressive," she murmurs. I hold out a hand to her and she takes it. I pull her up to stand beside me. She's so tiny that she barely comes up to my shoulder.

I reach over to adjust her shirt, but it's ripped all the way to her neckline. You can see her bra. I reach over my head and pull my shirt off the way guys do, ruck it up in my fingers, and slip it over her head.

"Thanks," she says. She lifts the neck of my shirt to her nose and takes a deep breath. "You smell really good." Suddenly, she looks around. "Where's Jason?"

She searches frantically until she finds him lying on the floor. She rushes over to him. "What happened?" she cries.

"I think that fucker broke my wrist," he says as he clutches his arm to his chest. He winces and she sinks down beside him.

"I'm so sorry," I hear her say.

"It's not your fault he was an asshole." He lays his head back against the wall and winces. "I think I need to go to the hospital."

She nods and helps him get up. "Should I call Norma?"

He nods. "If we don't, she'll never let me live it down. I'll be sleeping on the couch for a month."

Fin pulls his phone out of his pocket and gives him shit about finally getting to be close to his dick. He growls at her playfully, and ruffles her hair with his good hand.

By the time we get outside, Norma is there waiting at the curb with the car. "I can drive," Jason says.

"Get in the fucking car, Jason," Norma says as she holds the door open. She kisses Fin quickly and looks at me like she's wondering who I am and why I'm shirtless. She jerks a thumb toward me. "He's hot, Finny," she says. "Nice catch."

I see Fin mouth *I know, right?*

"Can you take her home?" Jason asks me.

"Of course," I rush to say. He looks fearful, so I try to reassure him. "We're only a few blocks from home."

"Don't let anything happen to her."

"I promise." I try to assure him, but he's still worried, I can tell. I think he truly cares about her.

"Can I go with you?" she asks him. "Please?" She's talking to Jason, not to me.

"Go home, Finny. I can't protect you tonight."

"I'll call you later, sweetie," Norma says. "I promise."

"You swear it?"

"Cross my heart and hope to die," Jason says.

"Well, don't die," Fin says. "I'd feel terrible. It would take me minutes to find Norma a better man."

Norma laughs and gets in the car. I watch as their taillights fade into the distance.

"Thanks for helping," she says quietly.

My breath makes little puffs in the cold night air. "You're welcome."

"So, what were you doing there?"

"Oh, shit." I thump the palm of my hand against my forehead. "I came to get you. They've been calling you for hours but you weren't answering."

She pulls her phone out of her pocket and scrolls through the texts.

"I totally forgot we go on tour tomorrow," she says on a groan.

I nod. I didn't forget. Wren says it's going to be a short tour, but we'll all be gone.

She starts walking quickly toward her apartment, her heels clicking on the concrete. She jams her hands into her pockets and I follow her.

"Finny," I say, after we get in the elevator at her apartment building.

"What?" She looks everywhere but at me.

"I thought we were going to go visit your mom this morning, but when I woke up you were gone. Did you change your mind?"

She shakes her head. "No. I went."

"By yourself?"

She nods.

"You were supposed to take me with you," I remind her.

She takes in a deep breath and lets it out. "She's fucking crazy, Tag. Totally mental. Like, locked-up-so-she-can't-kill-anybody mental. I don't like to take people to see that."

She's acting like this is new information for me. I already met her mom. I know what she's dealing with. "Was she okay today?"

She shakes her head. "No. She was herself." Her voice is quiet and I can barely hear her. She lays her head back against the wall of the elevator and closes her eyes.

Suddenly she opens them and looks at my bare chest. "Tag, can I tell you something?"

I cross my arms, because she's appraising my chest like she wants to have me for dinner. "I guess."

"You're fucking hot," she says. She licks her full lips, and I find myself going hard again.

Then the elevator dings, the doors open, and she steps out. I take a second and try to collect my wits, because they're scattered like a pocketful of dimes strewn around the floor. She reaches back and holds the door open.

"Bring your fine self inside," she says. She grins at me.

I wonder what she's like when she's not hiding her pain behind her sexuality. I suppose I won't have a chance to find out.

Finny

When I don't know what to do or how to comport myself, I flirt. It's how I've always gotten by. And watching Tag's face turn red, it's totally working. He's thinking more about kissing me than he is about my crazy mother.

I step into the living room and stop short. All four of my sisters are here.

Peck's sitting with her baby on her knee, and her husband Sam is next to her on the sofa.

My sister Star is sitting in her new husband's lap.

Wren and Lark are sharing an armchair, and Emilio and Marta are standing by the kitchen counter. "Where the hell have you been?" Emilio demands.

I look around at them all. "Dancing," I say slowly. "Why? What's up?" I go and get a bottle of water from the fridge.

"Why didn't you answer our calls, mija?" Marta asks.

I shrug. "I couldn't hear the phone over the music."

Suddenly, Emilio notices that Tag isn't wearing a shirt. "What happened?"

"Nothing," I say. I sit down on the arm of the couch. Tag goes and gets a shirt, and he's still pulling it over his head as he walks back into the room. As his most magnificent six-pack disappears, I see a streak of red, raw, angry skin disappear beneath the fabric. Was he hurt? I'll find out when the interrogation is over. "Where's the rugrat?"

Wren jerks her thumb toward Tag's room. "He's asleep."

Benji sleeps in tiny sprints, I've learned.

"His name is Benji," Tag reminds me.

"Benjamin Taggert the Third," my sisters all say in unison. Then they laugh when Tag scowls at them.

"Why are you wearing his shirt?" Emilio asks me again. He's not going to take no for an answer.

"Hers got torn off by an overzealous fan," Tag blurts out.

I mouth the word *traitor* at Tag. "It was nothing–"

"Jason is on the way to the hospital," Tag goes on to say. If he was two steps closer to me, I'd kick Tag in the nuts. "He was hurt. His wife picked him up."

"Are you okay?" Star asks Tag.

He waves a hand at her in dismissal. "I'm fine." Apparently, she didn't see the gash on his belly. The one that disappears into the sparse thatch of hair that leads to his rather impressive nether regions.

Emilio turns his back to me and starts to talk on the phone. He's probably getting the whole story from Jason right now, because he doesn't believe that it was nothing. But it was. It's normal when you're in a famous rock band. We're used to it. Sometimes the fans get too exuberant. It happens.

Emilio gets off the phone and goes to Tag. He holds out his hand for him to shake. Tag stares at it for a moment and then finally takes it in a handshake. He looks startled, though. "Thank you for bringing her home," Emilio says.

"No problem," Tag mutters.

"So, what's up with the group meeting?" I ask. I take a bag of chips from Lark and drop a handful of greasy goodness onto my shirt.

She snatches the bag back from me. "Get out of my chips," she snarls playfully.

I pick one up, lick all over it, and then hold it out to her. "Want it back?"

She pretends to heave and then tries to ignore me.

"So, the meeting?" I prompt again.

Emilio and Marta make eye contact with one another for a beat too long. "It's your mother," Emilio says.

I look from one to the other. "What about her?"

"She's worse, Finny," Emilio says, his voice so gentle that it's seriously pissing me off.

I snort. "That's nothing new."

"No," Emilio clarifies. "I mean she seriously hurt someone this afternoon. Another resident. They want to move her to a facility with more security."

I pop another chip into my mouth. "So?"

Marta huffs out a sigh. "So, mija, they need your permission to move her."

My mother has been in a long-term care facility since I was a little girl. They have to keep her in a place where they can regulate her meds. Usually, she's fine. Apparently, she now has more to worry about than her mental illness.

"You'll need to go and make some decisions about her care," he goes on to explain.

I shrug. "Why me?"

Marta comes to stand beside me and runs her hand down the length of my hair. "You're the only family she has left."

"So which one of you is going?" I grin at them. I have no desire to go and see my mother again. She was frantic today when I looked at her through the tiny glass in the door to her room. She paced from one side of the room to the other, wringing her hands, mumbling to herself.

"This is something *you* need to do," Marta says softly.

"Hire someone to go and evaluate my mother," I say with a shrug. "No biggie."

"We can't do that for you," Emilio says. "They also want to do some counseling with your mom and they would like for you to be present."

"No." *Hell no.*

"Finny—"

"*No*," I say again. "I'm not going. Besides, none of you can go with me, because we're booked for the tour. And Jason is in the hospital." I shrug. It seems so simple to me. I raise my finger in the air. "Speaking of which, if my personal security guard is injured, who's going to travel with me when we're on tour?"

Emilio and Marta look at one another, perplexed.

"I could go and help," a male voice says from the side of the room. I look up to find Tag leaning against the wall, his shoulder hitched in the doorway.

"You would do that?" Star asks.

He nods. "I was going anyway, to be a roadie." He laughs lightly.

"What about Benji?" says Wren.

He shrugs. "What about him? We'll take him with us." He points at Marta. "Marta said she was going to watch him while I worked. Now she won't have to. He can just hang with me."

"No." I say it quickly, and Tag's head spins around to face me. He's confused, but I can't have Tag following me everywhere for six tour dates.

"I can take care of you," Tag says.

The room goes quiet. You could hear a pin drop, if one should happen to do so.

"I don't need anyone to take care of me," I rush to say.

"Then it's settled." Emilio stands up and dusts his hands together.

"It's not settled!" I hiss.

But everyone is getting up from their seats. This is so *not* settled.

"Why aren't you listening to me?" I practically yell.

"You're going on tour and you have to have someone to protect you," Emilio says firmly. "Tag is going with you. Marta will help take care of the baby." He holds up his hands to stop me when I would interrupt. "That's all there is to it. Get your shit packed. You leave in the morning."

He's using the *dad voice* again. Damn it, I hate it when he does that. Emilio let us get away with a lot, but when he brought out the *dad voice*, we knew we had better listen.

"But–"

"No buts!" he says loudly. "It's settled, Finny. Go pack your shit." He points toward my room.

I get up, and I think about throwing the pillow I'm holding in my hands directly at his head, but I would never do it. I have too much respect for Emilio. But damn if it doesn't cross my mind.

Emilio chuckles as I stomp past him. "Don't even think about it."

I stick my middle finger up where he can't see it, just because I'm feeling defiant.

"I saw that!" he calls to my back.

I slam my bedroom door behind me and lean heavily against it. Then I start to pack my shit, because apparently I'm going on tour and I'm taking the man I had one night with along as security. Then I have to deal with my mother when we get back.

Fuck my life.

Tag

Finny slams her bedroom door and I scratch my head. Peck and Star take their husbands and go home, and Marta and Emilio hang out in the kitchen for a few minutes. Benji is stirring, so I go and fix him a bottle. He has been asleep for a while, and he's going to wake up hungry.

Emilio leans on the kitchen counter on his elbows and glares at me. I look behind me, because I can't think of any reason he would be staring at me like he hates me. I cough into my closed fist. "Is everything okay?" I ask him.

"Finny's special," he says.

I nod. "I'm sure she is."

"No, I mean really special."

I nod again, and pop Benji's bottle in the microwave.

"Finny's afraid of commitment," he says.

"Aren't we all," I mutter.

His brow arches, but he doesn't respond to that. "You'll take care of her while they're on tour, right?" he asks.

"I promise to do my best."

"I believe you." He points a finger at me. "But if you fuck it up, if she comes home with a single scratch on her body, I will murder you with my own two hands." He grins, but there's no humor in it. "You feel me?"

I swallow past the lump in my throat. "I feel you."

I shake the bottle, waiting for Benji to start making those little mewling noises.

"There are two things you should know about Finny," he says.

"Okay…"

"One, you have to listen to what she doesn't say, if you want to figure her out."

I nod.

"And two, never get between her and a coffee pot. She'll chop your balls off."

This much I already know about her, but I instinctively bend my back a little, and my nuts draw up. He laughs.

"Call me if you need anything," he says. He claps me on the shoulder and follows Marta to the door, after kissing his daughters goodbye.

"Night, Melio," Wren calls to him.

He waves at them and leaves.

Benji makes a noise from my room, so I take the bottle and go to him. I look down into his crib and see that he has kicked himself free of his swaddling blankets, and his skin is moist and rosy. I pick him up, talk to him as I change his diaper, and go back out to the rocking chair in the living room to sit with him.

Lark goes to bed, and Finny is still in her room, but Wren comes out to sit with me.

"So…" Wren says.

"So…"

"Do you think you can take care of Finny while we're on tour?" She bites her lower lip, worrying it.

"I'll do my best."

"Try not to fall in love with her, okay?"

I jerk my head up. "I won't."

"Oh, you will. But try not to, okay?"

"I can guarantee you that I'm not ready for a new relationship, Wren."

She heaves a sigh. "Neither is Fin. But seriously, Tag, don't fall in love with her. You'll just get hurt."

I look up at her. She's totally serious. "I can handle it."

She nods, but she still looks worried. "Don't say I didn't warn you." She gets up and goes to her room. She comes back out carrying a bank deposit receipt. "I put some more money in your account," she says. She tosses it onto the table.

"I don't want your money, Wren. Not now. I'm doing odd jobs for the Reeds and I'm okay. I really am. I just have to figure things out."

"Well, I don't want my nephew doing without while you figure it all out." She bends down and kisses Benji on the cheek. Then she shoves the side of my head with the heel of her hand. She reminds me so damn much of Mom right then that tears fill my eyes.

"You do look like her, you know?" I say. I sniffle back a tear.

"She was beautiful," Wren says softly.

"Yeah, she was."

She goes to her room and shuts the door.

As soon as she does, Finny's door opens and she stomps into the room. "Take off your shirt," she hisses.

"What?" I am startled by her bluntness.

"You were injured. I saw it." She points to my stomach, where Benji is resting. His mouth is slack around his bottle, so I pull it back and lay him on the couch beside me.

"I'm fine," I say. But I get up anyway.

"Show me."

I don't move, so she reaches out, lifts the edge of my shirt and draws it higher, exposing my stomach. "Oh, it's not bad," she says.

"Just a scratch, I think." I lower my shirt.

She goes to the bathroom and comes back with some antiseptic and cotton gauze. "Let me clean it."

I hold out my hand for the bottle. "I can do it."

She shakes her head. "I'll do it." She motions for me to take my shirt off, so I pull it over my head and toss it onto the couch beside us.

She pours antiseptic onto the gauze and starts to gently clean the area, but it burns like a bitch. I hiss loudly drawing in a breath.

"Oh, quit being such a baby," she chides. She bends down and blows across it, and I suppose she's trying to ease the sting. But the gentle feel of her breath on my skin starts a brand new kind of ache. My dick starts to press against my fly.

"I can do it," I say. I try to turn, but she grabs my belt loop and holds me still. I close my eyes and think about cheeseburgers. Warts. Ice. But then my ice turns into a drop of water melting and sliding down her skin in my lust-filled mind. Oh, holy hell. "I can do it," I say again.

Suddenly she notices the bulge behind my fly. "Oh," she says, her cheeks turning rosy. "Whoops." She giggles and shoves the first aid supplies into my hands. "Didn't, um, mean to, um, cause that." She waves a hand toward my dick. "I mean, we can't do that again."

"We totally should," I tell her, my voice gravelly. "I mean, if you ever drop your moratorium against sleeping with someone twice."

She nods at me, her gaze once more falling to my dick, which is still standing at attention. "Tempting," she offers. She grins at me. "You might need help with that."

I roll my eyes. "I can handle it, thanks."

"If you say so." She turns and goes to her room. At the last moment, she turns back to me. "What time do you want to leave in the morning? I need to go talk to my mother's doctor before we leave, and I guess you're going with me."

"Whenever you get up."

She nods. "I guess we can't say whenever *you* get up, since, well…" She grins at me.

"Beautiful *and* funny," I mutter.

She lays a hand on her chest. "Did you just call me *funny?*" She bats her lashes at me.

"Among other things."

She shrugs. "I like funny better." Then she goes into her room, the door softly clicking closed behind her.

"Yeah, I do too," I murmur to no one.

I think I'm in trouble. Big trouble.

Finny

Two cups of coffee is not enough. Tag doesn't seem to mind my bitchiness, though. He walks solemnly beside me down the sidewalk. I take a deep breath, because for the first time ever, I want to tell someone about my mom.

"The first time my mother ever tried to kill me, we were on a Ferris wheel at the county fair. She was cycling, I know now. I didn't know it then. I just though we were going to have a fun day. My mother had days that were really low, but every now and then she would have an up day. And when she was up, she was flying. She had an imagination and she wanted to go on adventures and we laughed and played."

Tag walks along beside me and doesn't say anything. He just listens.

"But I was six the first time she ever tried to kill me."

I sink into the memory like it was yesterday.

"I don't want to go," I whispered to her, as we stood in line for the Ferris wheel.

She squatted down next to me. "What did you say, sweetie?"

"I don't want to go," I said again, this time a little louder.

She stood back up, still holding tightly to my hand. "Oh, everyone needs to ride the Ferris wheel, sweetie." She spread her arms out wide. "The world looks so big from up there."

I tugged on her hand again. "I don't want to go."

But she was already passing our tickets to the carnival worker. She jerked my arm and yanked me onto the platform. I followed her, because she was squeezing my hand so hard it hurt. There was a frantic look in her eye, and I knew that our up day was over. She was on the way back down and crashing hard.

And she was going to take me with her.

We got in the seat and the carnival worker clamped the long bar across our laps, but my legs were so small that it barely held me in. The contraption rocked as it began to rotate, and I grabbed the bar as tight as I could. Mom leaned over the edge and looked down. "Look, baby."

I squeezed my eyes shut. I didn't want to look.

The seat rocked again as more people got on. "Look," she said again. She yelled it this time, and I saw the people in the bucket above us look down at us with a frown. I wanted to tell them I was fine, but I was not fine. I was not ever going to be fine.

The rocking stopped and we started to move in a slow circle. I squeezed my eyes shut.

"Open your eyes," Mom said.

The wind very gently blew my hair back, and I was glad I'd let her put the pretty pink bows in my hair before we left home that morning.

"I said open your eyes," Mom snarled. She squeezed my chin between her thumb and forefinger and I let out a cry. "Are you afraid to fall?" she asked. She held her arms out to the side and closed her eyes, her face contrary to what was going on in her head. She confused me so much when she got like this. "Are you afraid to fall?" she asked again, this time louder.

"No," I said quietly. I was much more afraid to be in that bucket with her.

Suddenly, she grabbed the front of my dress and lifted me from my seat onto her lap. The bar was so loose that it provided no resistance at all. I wrapped my arms around her neck.

"I'm going to teach you an important life lesson, sweetie," she said, her voice close to my ear.

"No!" I struggled to hold on to her, but she pried my arms away from her neck as she turned me upside down. She held me by my feet over the back of the basket, and I flailed, trying to find something to hold on to. "Mommy!" I screamed.

The people below me started to freak out, and the ride stopped entirely.

"This is what falling feels like!" Mom cried. "Remember what this feels like, baby, so you'll never do anything so stupid."

"Pull me up," I pleaded. Her hands faltered, slippery with sweat, and I slid down a little. The ride had stopped and the man in the bucket below us held out his arms like he might be able to catch me if she did drop me. "Please! Mommy! Pull me up!"

She laughed. "Falling, baby. Make sure you never do it."

"I won't!" I shouted tearfully. I watched as my pretty pink hair bows fell from my hair and landed in the grass far below us. "I promise I'll never ever fall."

Finally, she pulled me up and I scurried to the edge of the bench, trying to stay as far from her as I could. She tossed her head back and laughed.

The ride started back up, and we finally got to the bottom. There were two police officers waiting when we got off, and one of them took my hand while the other put handcuffs on my mom.

The next three months I got to stay with my grandmother. I was safe with my grandmother. I was happy with my grandmother. No one tried to kill me when I was with my grandmother.

But when they got my mom's meds regulated, they sent me back to her. This happened over and over until I was ten, and my grandmother died. Then I had no one to take me, and I was officially in the system.

That was the best day of my life. The day I went to a group home because there was nowhere else for me to go. That was the day my life started.

But there is one thing I know for sure. My mom taught me a lesson that day. "Don't ever fall, baby. Never, ever fall." So I don't. And I won't. I can't.

I will never step close to the edge. I'll never get myself into that kind of situation.

I jerk myself out of my trance when Tag puts his arm around me and pulls me into an alley. "Sixty seconds," he says.

He pulls me against him and I go willingly. He holds me tightly, and I relish every second. I don't know when I started to need this man, but I'm there.

He gets to sixty and sets me back, but this time he does it slowly, almost like he doesn't want to let me go.

"My mom is batshit crazy," I tell him as I step back into the street and we walk toward the assisted living facility. He left Benji with Wren, and I'm kind of glad. I'd be afraid my mother would hurt him.

He nods. "Sounds like it."

We go in, and I sign the paperwork so the administrators can move her to a section of the facility that has more security. "Is that all you need from me?" I ask as I push the clipboard back toward the doctor in charge.

"We'd like to offer some counseling for you and your mom. I know it wasn't always easy for you." He's the psychiatrist who is responsible for my mom's treatment.

I shake my head. "What good would that do?"

"Honestly? For her, probably nothing. For you, maybe it would help."

"I'm fine," I say.

He nods. "Let me know if you change your mind."

Tag and I step back onto the sidewalk outside and he says, "You didn't want to see her?"

I shake my head. "No." I heave a sigh.

He looks straight at me and stares into my eyes. "You still have hope that she'll love you the way you need to be loved?"

"No. I stopped hoping for that a long time ago."

"I don't believe you," he says. His hand slips into mine, and he tangles our fingers together. I close my eyes and take a deep breath, but I don't pull my hand away. "Do you feel like having breakfast?"

I nod, and we go into a small place that specializes in waffles.

He opens a menu. "What's good here?" he asks. He grins at me.

"Duh," I say. "Waffles."

He lays the menu to the side. "Then I guess I'll have waffles." He looks up at the waitress. "And coffee."

"Same," I say.

"So, you're afraid of heights now?" he asks as he stirs cream into his coffee.

"No, I'm just afraid of falling."

He stares hard at me over the rim of his mug. "Explain."

"I have to have my feet solidly planted, that's all."

His eyes narrow. "You like control."

I nod and give a little shrug. "Yes."

"So when you and I were together…" He stops and shakes his head. "Never mind." His cheeks turn red.

"Say it," I prompt. My heart is tripping like mad.

"When we were together and I slapped your ass, did it turn you on or did it turn you off?"

My palms start to sweat, so I wipe them on my jeans. "I've had men slap my ass before."

His jaw muscle jerks. "We're not talking about them. We're talking about you and me."

I sit back and try to breathe. "So, you want to know if you turned me on?"

"Yes."

"Why do you care?" I watch his face closely.

"Because I fully intend to do it again one day, when you're ready for what I want."

My belly betrays me with a little flip. "And what do you want?"

"I want to wait while I get to know you. And I want to take you on a few dates. And I want for you to fall in love with me and with my son. And then, when we're both sure we want it, I want to fuck you again, but this time it'll be more. So much more."

I can't speak. I didn't expect him to lay his cards on the table like this. I expected him to cover his hand and protect it, just like I would do. "I don't fuck anybody more than once."

"I know. That's why I don't want that. I want to make you fall in love with me." He takes my hand in his and drags his thumb across the back of it in slow sweeps.

"You don't want much, do you?"

He shakes his head, the corners of his mouth quirking just a little. "I want it all."

"With me?"

He nods. "With you."

"Can I think about it?"

He shakes his head. "No. If you think too much, you'll run scared."

"So what should I do?"

"Let me love you." He shrugs. "That's all."

I scoff. "You don't love me."

He grins. "Not yet. But I want to date you." He squeezes my hand. "Will you go on a date with me, Finny?"

I look around the restaurant. "Aren't we doing that now?"

He smiles. "Are we?"

"Maybe," I whisper.

The waitress arrives with our waffles, and he lets my hand go. He eats in silence, and so do I.

When we're done, he pulls out his wallet.

"I got it," I say. I pull a credit card from my pocket.

"I pay," he says.

"Dude, do you know how much money I made last year?"

"I pay, Finny."

I flounce back against the seat. "Why?"

"I don't have much, but I earned what I do have, and I want to spend it on you. So let me, okay?" He stares hard at me. "Let me value you. Treasure you. Enjoy you. Treat you the way you should be treated. You can trust me, Finny. I won't let you fall."

A lump forms in my throat and I swallow hard to push past it.

"Thank you for breakfast," is all I can say.

He signs the check and we get up. He tangles his fingers with mine again and we walk side by side down the street. "Can I feed Benji when we get home?" I ask quickly. Heat creeps up my cheeks when he grins at me.

"You don't like babies," he reminds me. He bumps my arm playfully with his.

"I like you. And I might like your baby. I have to spend some time with him to see."

He nods. "Okay," he says. "You can feed him. I need to pack, anyway."

We walk side by side, hand in hand, and I am afraid that I'm falling way too fast. I swore I would never, ever fall, but this doesn't feel like freefalling. This feels like soaring. Like catching the wind and letting it carry me.

"Would you really catch me if I fell?" I ask him as we step into the elevator.

He pulls me against him and his lips hover over mine. "I'd catch you, or I'd fall with you trying to keep you up."

"Don't set me up, okay?" I lay my forehead against his chest so he can't see the truth in my eyes. I don't want him to see how much I want this. How much I want him. How much I want the perfect.

"I won't." He tips my face up and his lips touch mine, tentative and slow at first, but then he spins us around and presses me against the wall, holding my face in his hands. His lips are suddenly hard, and his tongue slips into my mouth. He tastes like waffle syrup and heat. He's breathless when he steps back, and I see him adjust his junk.

"You okay?" I blink down toward his discomfort.

"I'm fine." He grins. "He'll give up in a second."

I laugh out loud. "I hope not."

When the door opens I step out of the elevator and he follows, then pulls me back against his front, his arms around me, his hand on my belly. He holds me and whispers in my ear. "I think I'm in like, Finny."

I cover his hand with mine. "Me too," I whisper. He kisses my cheek quickly and we go inside the apartment.

He's going to break my heart. And I'm going to let him, because for the first time ever, it might be okay to be vulnerable, at least with him.

Tag

Four days on a tour bus with a woman I have a serious crush on, and now my body aches too much to even put the moves on her.

"Sam!" I call out across the lawn where we're setting up their stage. "Where do you want this?" I point to the speaker I'm holding.

"Up your ass would be fine," he yells back at me. He grins, though, so I'm pretty sure he's joking.

I set the speaker down and wait for instructions.

He walks over to me and claps me on the shoulder. "We can let the set-up crew finish the rest of this."

"You sure? I can keep going," I tell him. I'm lying, but still.

"Well, I can't. I plan to fuck my wife later, and my back isn't going to let me if we don't quit soon."

"Well, there's that," I say. My face floods with heat.

He stares at me, his eyes narrowed, and then shakes his head.

"What?"

"Nothing."

"No, it's something. Say it."

"What's going on with you and Finny?" he asks.

I shrug. "Nothing. Why?" I look everywhere but at him.

"Because," he says slowly, "she's my family, and I want to be sure you're in it for the right reasons."

"And what reasons would those be?"

"The good kind. Not just the I-want-to-get-in-her-pants kind."

"I have good intentions. *And* the I-want-to-get-in-her-pants intentions. And the I-want-to-make-her-fall-madly-in-love-with-me intentions."

His eyes open wide. "Damn. You're one pussy-whipped bastard."

"You're right." He's right. I am pussy-whipped. I watched her walk by me this afternoon, and she winked at me once, and it was all I could do not to chase her down so I could kiss her right then and there, in front of everybody. "You think I have a shot?"

I sit down on the speaker and he sits beside me.

"Finny's a strange bird," he replies. I open my mouth to protest, but he shushes me. "Hang on," he says. "Finny's amazingly talented as a musician. She's fierce on those strings, but she's afraid of everything."

"She doesn't act like she's afraid of anything."

"She's a good actor, too." He points a finger at me. "But as long as you have good intentions, I'll leave you two alone."

I nod. "You have nothing to worry about. My intentions are honorable." Well, I kind of would like to get in her pants, too, but still honorable.

"Just be easy with her," he says. He pinches his lips together. "I take that back," he says. "Don't be easy with her. If you pussyfoot around, she'll never tell you how she feels."

"How do you think she feels?" I ask him.

"I think she likes you a lot." He points over my shoulder. "She can't take her eyes off you."

All the girls and Emily are standing on the stage, and they're testing the microphones and stage equipment. Finny holds up her thumb to show that her setup is okay. She looks over at me and smiles and I lose my breath a little bit.

"I'm not worried about your intentions anymore," Sam says quietly.

"Why not?"

"Because when she smiled at you, you looked like the happiest guy in the world." He grins at me. "Congratulations."

Marta walks around the corner and she's pushing a double stroller. Sammy, Sam's two-month-old, is in one bucket seat and my son is in the other. She stops in front of us. "I've decided to keep both the boys tonight so you guys can get some rest," she says.

My brow shoots up. "What?"

She grins at me. "It's purely selfish. I like the little guy, and he likes me, and I think you need a break."

"I can't ask you to do that," I object.

"You're not asking. I'm telling you."

"Are you sure?" My heart leaps in my chest at the thought of a night of uninterrupted sleep.

"Emilio and I got a hotel room so we would have space for the cribs." She winks at me. "Enjoy a night with no babies or parents on the bus."

My face gets hot. Surely she's not suggesting…

"Dude, I think she just told you to go get laid," Sam says, leaning his head toward mine.

"She did not."

He grins. "She totally did."

Marta turns back to face me. "She totally did," she says. She smiles at me again. "I may be old, but I'm not dead."

I lean down and kiss my son on the forehead. He turns his head like he wants to nurse on my cheek, and I let him nuzzle for a minute. God, he has my heart. "I'll see you tomorrow," I tell him. I kiss him, lingering over his tender skin a moment longer than I should, I know. "Call me if you need anything?" I tell Marta.

"Of course." She steps up onto her tiptoes and kisses my cheek really quickly. Then she says quietly so only I can hear it, "Finny's afraid to sleep with a man."

Finny has slept with a lot of men, I think.

"Sleeping with a man is so much more intimate than having sex with one." She stares hard at me. "You know?" Then she walks away and takes my son with her.

"Dude, can you give me about twenty minutes before you come to the bus?" Sam asks me.

Seriously, he's asking me to stay away so he can make love to his wife? I grin at him. "It takes you twenty minutes?"

"No, today it'll take me two, but I'll give her twenty, if you can stay away."

"You got it." I look down at my watch. "Starting now."

Sam walks over to Peck, whispers in her ear, takes her hand in his, and pulls her toward the bus. She laughs and pretends to struggle, but he won't take no for an answer. Finally, he wraps his arm around her and guides her, with her laughing all the while.

Finny looks so damn pretty standing there on the stage that I can't stay away from her. I walk up slowly, and go to her. She's with Emily and Logan. I don't know Logan very well, but I know he's pretty easy to talk to. He has a cochlear implant he just got, but he had pretty good speech even before that, from what I understand. I walk up to Finny and put my hand at the center of her back. She leans into me without even thinking about it, and it makes my heart go all trippy.

"You have plans tonight?" I ask her. I press my lips to her temple and linger there. Her eyes flutter closed for a second.

"Nope. You?" She gazes at me shyly.

"You want to go to dinner with me?" My heart is racing for some reason.

She reaches up, cups my face in her palm, and stares into my eyes. "Aren't you tired?"

"Not too tired to show you how much I want to spend time with you," I admit. "Never too tired for that." I lift her hand from my face and press my lips to her palm. The hair on her arms stands up.

"How about if we go get pizza and take it back to the bus?" Her voice quivers.

"Okay." I lean down close to her ear. "We're supposed to give Sam and Peck twenty minutes, anyway. I promised."

She snorts. "It won't take Sam twenty minutes."

I pull my head back so I can look down at her. "How would you know that?"

She shrugs. "Girls talk." Her cheeks get rosy.

"Did you talk with them about me?"

"I told them exactly how big your dick is and that it hooks a little to the left."

My heart stops. "It does not."

She shoves my shoulder. "I'm kidding. The only one who knows about us is Lark. And that's because she caught you coming out of my room. I didn't tell her anything. Well, not about how your dick made me sore or anything."

I grin. "I made you sore?"

"And you left your handprint on my ass."

"It was gone before I even left that night."

She stares into my eyes. "It'll be there forever in my mind."

I lean down and kiss her quickly. "Mine too."

"So, pizza?"

I nod, and she slips her hand into mine. "I think there's a place about two blocks from here. We'll walk." She reaches over, takes the ball cap from my head, and puts it on hers. "Don't want to be recognized," she explains.

She looks so damn cute in my ball cap that I don't think I'll ever take it back. She grins at me so I grab the brim and wiggle it on her head. Her grin turns into a smile with teeth.

"I really like you," I blurt out.

Her smile tips up even bigger. "I like you too."

"Will you do me a favor?"

"Depends on what it is," she says, her gaze skeptical.

"Don't make me fall in love with you unless you're capable of loving me back, okay?"

She inhales quickly, and I panic for a moment. But then she steps onto her tiptoes and kisses me, and I know she feels it too. I can tell. The vice around my heart eases a little.

"Pizza," she murmurs against my lips.

"Yes," I mumble against her skin.

Suddenly, someone kicks the back of my knee and I stumble. "What the…" I turn around and find Logan staring at me.

"Emily and I are getting a room tonight," he says. "Her mom and dad are in town and they have Kit."

I nod. "Okay. Thanks for the heads up."

He smiles. "Have fun."

I try not to grin too much. "We're not quite there yet."

"That's why I said have fun instead of have lots of sex." He shoves my shoulder and walks by us.

"So, it's just me and you, and Sam and Peck in the bus tonight?" Finny says. There's a second bus for the others.

"Looks like it."

"Why don't you all get hotel room?" I ask her.

She shrugs. "We like the bus. It becomes like home after you've been traveling for a while." She waits a beat.

"So we won't be alone tonight," she says.

"Nope." I stare into her eyes long enough to make her cheeks flush.

She smiles shyly at me but she doesn't say anything more.

We go and get pizzas and she fights with me so I'll let her pay for them. "Everyone is going to eat them!" she tells me. "Not just us. I'm not letting you buy for all of us. The band has a budget for this stuff."

"Then let me at least buy mine."

"You're part of the band, doofus."

Laughter bubbles from my throat. "Did you just call me a doofus?"

"Maybe." Then she starts to laugh too. I give her time to calm down while I take her card and pay for the pizzas. Then we start back to the bus. "I'm really glad you're here," she says. She puts her hand in my back pocket.

"You keep that up and I'm going to give up on being a gentleman," I warn playfully.

She squeezes my ass and I jump, almost upending the pizzas.

"You're going to get me in so much trouble," I tell her. But I welcome it. I've never felt quite so alive. Not until I started spending time with her.

We go back to the bus and she opens the door. We climb quickly up the steps because, honestly, I want to put the pizzas down so I can grab her and pull her against me.

But when we get in the bus, she screams and turns to face me really quickly. "Oh, my God, Sam!" she cries. "Are you serious? Put that thing away. Oh my God. Oh my God. Oh my God," she chants to herself, her hands over her eyes as she buries her face in my chest.

"Sorry," Sam says. "We didn't think you'd be back for a few more minutes."

Sam and Peck rush to put their clothes back on. I see way too much of Sam's ass as he turns to cover Peck up with his own width. "You said you needed twenty. We gave you thirty," I tell him. I look out the front window of the bus. Everywhere but at them, because I just saw way too much of Sam. Peck we could only see from the backside—and a really pretty backside it was—but Sam...Sam was balls deep.

"Well, when you didn't come back after twenty, we decided to do it again. Sue me for being excited about having my wife all to myself." Sam pulls his shirt over his head and pulls his pants up from where they were resting around his ankles.

"Sorry," Peck says. "You didn't really see anything, did you?" She looks from me to Finny and back.

"I didn't see a thing," I say.

She doesn't look like she believes me.

"Can I talk to you for a second?" Finny asks her. "Outside?"

"Are you okay?" I ask Finny.

"I think I'll be scarred for life," she whispers back to me. But she's grinning.

She and Peck go out the door of the bus. Sam reaches for the pizza box. "Dude, go wash your hands," I tell him, snatching the box away.

"Seriously?"

I glare at him. "Seriously."

He mutters all the way to the sink. "If I want to eat with my wife's pussy on my hands, I should be able to do that."

"You can when it's your own pizza," I toss back.

He chuckles. "Hey, don't tell Peck you saw anything, will you? She'll flip the fuck out."

"Mums the word," I tell him. But I do know he's one lucky dude.

Finny

"Oh my God," I'm still chanting when the bus door closes behind us.

Peck scowls at me. "Finny, it's not like you've never seen a penis before."

"I've never seen a great big penis in a position where it might be partially buried in your vagina," I toss back.

She laughs. "Don't tell Sam you saw his dick, okay? He'll get a complex."

"That man has nothing to be ashamed of, Peck. How the fuck do you fit all that up in there?"

She laughs so hard she snorts. "Well, it's hard, but we make it work."

I burst out laughing. I laugh so hard that it takes me a minute to calm down.

"Well, I can never un-see that, just so you know."

She shrugs. "His dick is a magical thing. I'm not ashamed." She narrows her eyes at me. "So, what did you want?"

I play with a loose string on my sleeve, trying to compose my thoughts. "I don't think I want to sleep with him."

She shrugs. "So don't."

"Do you think he'd mind?" I nibble on my lower lip.

"Who cares if he minds, Finny?" she asks me softly. "Are you worried that all he wants is sex?"

I take a deep breath. "No, I'm worried that's *not* all he wants. I'd know what to do with him if he just wanted sex."

"Oh," she breathes. "So that's it. You really like him."

"Yeah," I whisper.

"What do you like most about him?"

"He knows about my crazy mother and he doesn't seem to care. He also knows about all my one-nighters. And he still likes me. At least I think he likes me. Do you think he likes me?"

"I think he likes you a lot," she says softly. "Oh, Finny…" She starts to blink frantically.

"Are you crying? Seriously?" I offer her my sleeve and she wipes her eyes on it.

"I can't help it. You're falling in love."

I contradict her quickly. "No, I'm not."

She gives me an incredulous look.

"I'm really not," I rush to tell her.

"Finny, you're acting like a total girl," she says softly.

"Is this what girls do?" I bite my fingernail while I wait for her answer.

"This is what people do, dummy. They question relationships when they're real. You're having a real relationship for the first time ever." She sniffles. "I'm so happy for you."

"So, do you think Sam could keep his dick in his pants from here on out?" I ask her, trying to ease some of the tension that's hanging around us.

She lifts her shoulders. "Maybe. I'll file the request for you."

"So just how big *is* your vagina?"

"Big enough," she says on an exaggerated huff.

"Well, that was apparent."

She laughs. "Fuck you, Finny."

"I'd return the sentiment, but Sam already did. I had ringside seats."

She giggles and turns to go back into the bus. She grabs a piece of pizza and slides into the booth seat next to Sam. I scoot in next to Tag and do the same. I lay my hand on his thigh and give it a squeeze. His free hand immediately covers mine and holds it tight. I look up at him to find him smiling down at me.

"So, Sam," Tag says, clearing his throat.

Sam looks up. "What?"

"How much did that piercing hurt?" He says it with a straight face.

But I can't control my laughter. I laugh so hard I choke on a piece of sausage and Tag has to pound me on the back.

"Dude, I could hook you up with a piercing," Sam says. "I'm a certified hole puncher at the tattoo shop."

"I am not letting you put any holes in my dick."

I cover my mouth to keep from laughing out loud. "Would you let me do it?" I ask him. I don't even know where that came from. Oh, shit.

He stares into my eyes. "I'd let you do just about anything you wanted to do, Finny," he says. He brushes a lock of hair back from my eyes. "I'm pretty sure you'd never hurt me on purpose."

"I wouldn't," I say.

Sam makes a gagging noise from his side of the table and Peck elbows him in the side. "What?"

"Stop giving them a hard time," she scolds. "I think it's sweet."

Peck makes Sam get up, and says, "I'm going to feed Sammy one last time before we go to sleep."

Sam wipes his mouth. "I'll go with you."

"Should I go and feed Benji?" Tag asks.

Sam points to Peck's boobs. "Dude, she's got the bottles."

"Oh," Tag says, his face turning red. "Forgot about that."

"Marta will take care of Benji," Peck assures him. "I'll look in on him while I'm there if you want."

Tag nods. "That would be great. Thanks."

They leave, and Tag wraps his palm around the back of my neck and pulls me to him so he can kiss me. "So, how long do you think they'll be gone?"

"Not that long. Sammy eats quick." I open my mouth when he teases my lips with his tongue and I sigh into his mouth. He has me breathless in seconds. "I had better get to bed," I say, but my heart is racing.

He looks toward the tiny bunk beds in the back of the bus. They're no bigger than coffins.

"Do you want the top or the bottom?" I ask.

"Why, Finny, did you just proposition me?" He lays a hand on his chest and pretends to be shocked.

I shake my head and grin. "No, I just wanted to know which bed I should crawl into."

"Mine," he says quickly.

My heart thuds. "I don't think so."

"Fine. You go pick one, and I'll crawl in with you." He starts to clean up the pizza while I go wash off my makeup, brush my teeth, and brush out my hair.

I climb into the bottom bunk and pull the privacy curtain behind me. "Good night, Tag," I call out.

The curtain shifts and I see his head appear. "Can I come in?" he asks. He waits in the opening for me to decide.

"I've never…"

"I know," he says softly. "I get it." He looks at me a beat too long and I have to look away. There's so much want in his eyes that I don't know what to do with it all. "Can I come in?"

I nod and he pulls back. I hear his jeans rustle as he slips them off, and then he goes and brushes his teeth. He comes back to the bed and climbs in beside me. There's barely enough room for one, much less two. He bangs his head on the roof. "Ouch," he cries.

I roll onto my side, trying to make more room for him, but he's a big guy. "I don't think you'll fit," I tell him on a silly, frantic giggle.

"I'll fit. I promise." He wiggles until he's flat on his back and then he lifts an arm and draws me in to his side. He points to the spot where his shoulder meets his arm. "Your head, it goes here."

I remember when we had sex and I told him where his dick went. "Okay," I say, and I settle into the spot, rooting around until I find the perfect place to rest my face. "I'm scared," I whisper. "I've never done this before." My heart is pounding and my skin is clammy.

He kisses my forehead, his lips lingering for a beat too long. "I won't hurt you, Finny," he whispers.

He grabs my leg and pulls it across his lap, and I can feel the ridge of his dick. He's hard. "Did you want to—" I start to ask.

But he shushes me. "I'm doing exactly what I want to do."

He holds me close until my shivers stop and my heart slows its frantic pace. I melt against him and close my eyes.

"I've never done this before. I might be bad at it," I whisper in the darkness.

"You're definitely not bad at it."

After a few minutes, I start to yawn. "Hey, Tag," I whisper.

"Hey, Finny," he whispers back.

"You're really good at this," I tell him.

"It's all you, Finny," he says. "All you."

Tag

I wake up in the early morning to the feel of the bus rocking. It's just a gentle bump, but I still blink my eyes open and look out the tiny window. The sun is just barely up over the horizon. Finny giggles in my arms and I look down at her.

"They're like rabbits," she whispers, scooting up so she can speak quietly by my ear.

"What's like rabbits?" I scrub a hand down my face and try to wake up.

"Sam and Peck."

"Oh. That's them?"

"Screwing. Again." She rolls her eyes and presses her lips against my chin. "Good morning." She nuzzles her head against my neck.

My dick is hard and I have people four feet from me going at it like they haven't seen one another in a year. Peck starts to make quiet little noises that make me want to stick my fingers in my ears and sing out lalalalalalalalala.

Finny lifts herself up and straddles my hips, her chest flush against mine. "Do you want me to take your mind off of it?"

I hold her face in my hands and look into her eyes. "What did you have in mind?" She kisses me softly. She tastes like morning and awesome all rolled into one tiny body. "That'll work," I mumble when she finally lifts her head. My brain feels like mush and I realize I'm kiss-drunk.

Peck's noises grow and then crest, and I close my eyes tightly, trying to drown out the sounds. But Finny shouts like she's at a ballgame and sits up a little in the tiny space so she can clap. "Hell yeah!" she says. "Nice work, Sam!"

Finny opens the curtain on our side a little and Sam opens the curtain on his, and they high-five in the middle. Peck's head sticks out sheepishly. "Sorry," she says, her cheeks rosy. "We didn't know you were awake."

"Well, it's kind of hard to sleep through all that noise," Finny says. "And the rocking."

"The bus was rocking?" Peck asks Sam.

"Hell yeah, the bus was rocking," he says on a chuckle. Then he pulls the curtain shut again.

"How do you think they did that in such a tiny space?" I whisper in Finny's ear.

She rocks her hips a little and says, "I think we could make it work." She giggles when I grab her hips to keep her still. If she keeps that up, I'll embarrass us both.

She reaches down between us and wraps her fist around my dick. I hiss in a breath.

"Shh," she whispers.

"Don't, Finny." I grab for her hand and try to stop her. She pulls her hand back up and rocks her heat against my dick. "Don't do that, either," I say.

I roll so that I dump her into the tiny spot beside me and we face one another on our sides. I slip my fingers under her t-shirt so I can cup her naked hip. She kisses me and it shoots straight to my toes, and my heart starts to trip.

I lift my head and groan. "I should get up."

She reaches down and slides her hand into my boxers, wrapping her tight little fist around me. "Some parts of you are already up," she says impishly.

"Finny," I complain quietly. I don't want Sam and Peck to hear me beg.

"I want to come so bad," she whispers in my ear.

I freeze. "You do?"

She nods.

"Well, damn," I say. "Let me help you out."

"No…" she says slowly, staring into my eyes. "We're not ready."

I slide my hand up her side, slowly lifting her shirt. "This okay?"

She rucks her shirt up over her boobs in answer to my question.

"So pretty." I groan and bury my face in her soft skin, dropping kisses here and there. Then she cups her boob in her hand and pulls my head toward her pert nipple.

She takes in a quick breath when I lap at it with my tongue. I give it a quick suck, and the sound of her breath nearly has me coming in my boxers. I nibble and kiss and suck until she's squirming in my arms. Her nipples have been kissed hard-tight and they strain against my chest when I pull her against me.

"Can I touch you?" I ask. I hover over the waist of her pants, my palm flat against her belly, my fingers pointing toward her heat.

"Please," she says. I slide my fingers into her panties and work my way between her lower lips, finding her hot and wet and slippery-sweet. She kisses me while I find her clit, and she bites down gently on my lower lip and stops moving when I find the right spot.

"Right there?" I whisper.

She nods.

I rub in a small circle, guided by the movement of her hips.

Then I feel her pull out the waistband of my boxers. I freeze for a second, waiting to see what she's going to do. She holds my waistband out with one hand and spits into the other, and then wraps her slick fingers around my dick.

My mouth falls open and I have to remind myself not to make noise. She pushes me to start moving my fingers against her clit again when she rocks her hips. She kisses me, smothering my raspy exhales. It's only seconds later and I'm ready to come, but I hold back. Her breaths are quick against my lips, and she makes a little noise. It grows slightly louder, but I'm pretty sure only she and I can hear it. It's the sweetest sound I've ever heard. Suddenly, she cups my face with the hand that's not wrapped around my dick and she looks into my eyes.

Then she comes apart in my arms. I spill into her tiny little fist, and she smears the head of my dick with it and keeps pumping, while she shivers and trembles in my hold. I stroke her, growing softer as her body eases a little. "Wow," she says, when we're both still.

"Yeah." I bury my face in her shoulder, kissing her collarbone, and working my way up her neck to her face. "Wow," I say like an idiot.

Suddenly, we hear clapping from the other bed. "Hell yeah!" Sam calls out. He does a few cat-calls, and I feel Finny bury her face in my chest. I palm the back of her hair and ask her if she's all right.

Her head shakes against me and I realize she's laughing. "At least we didn't rock the bus," she says loudly.

"Not everybody can be as awesome as me," Sam crows.

"I don't know," Finny whispers to me. "That was pretty amazing."

She fixes her panties and rolls over the top of me to get out of bed. She comes back with damp hands from where she just washed them and passes me a warm wet cloth. I clean up really quickly and she throws it into a hamper.

She climbs back into bed with me and puts her head on my chest. "Can we go back to sleep?" she asks.

I nod and hold her close to me. "You didn't have to do that," I tell her.

"I know." She kisses the stubble on my chin. "That's what made it so wonderful."

She settles against me. Our heartbeats collide. I finally have the key to that door labeled Happiness, and it's standing right there, gaping wide open in front of me.

Finny

Tag is still under me, and he's making little soft snuffly noises. I ease off of him slowly, trying not to wake him. He shifts, and I pause my movement until he settles again. I open the curtain and back out of the tiny space. I clean up really quickly and put on some clothes that might look presentable.

I leave a note for Tag so he won't be surprised when he wakes up and finds me gone. I tell him where I'll be and hope he comes and finds me.

Then I leave the bus and go to the hotel on the corner. I know which room Marta and Emilio are in, and I knock softly on their door. Marta greets me there and I see her gently bouncing Peck's baby on her shoulder.

"That one wants his mommy, huh?" I ask her.

"I'm trying to hold him off because I know she'll want to feed him."

Sammy is sucking on his little fists. I hold out my arms to take him. He comes to me and I pop a pacifier into his mouth, but he'll have none of it. He's getting more and more fretful.

I text Peck really quickly and tell her if she doesn't come and feed her baby quickly, I'm going to give him a bottle.

BE RIGHT THERE, she texts back.

"She's on the way," I tell Marta. I look around and see Benji asleep in his portable crib. "Did you get any sleep last night?"

She yawns. "Not much. One or the other was up most of the night." She smiles at me though. "How was your night?"

"Good," I say cryptically.

"Oh, yeah?" she asks. She grins wide. "How good?"

"We didn't do anything," I whisper, my cheeks growing hot.

"I think you're lying, mija," she says. "I think you did *everything*."

I blush. "Yeah, we kind of did…" I squeeze my eyes shut tight. "And it was wonderful."

She just smiles at me.

"Where's Melio?" I ask.

She nods toward the bedroom. "He's sleeping. He helped with the grandbabies last night."

I grin. "He did?"

"He has decided that he wants to be called Melio instead of Grandpa."

I shrug. "That fits."

She shrugs too. "I don't think anyone will care. You girls never called him Daddy. It was always Melio."

"Yeah, but he knows he's Dad in our hearts."

"He does." She smiles.

Benji starts to stir, so I go and get him and change his diaper. I'm all thumbs because I haven't done it much, but Marta helps me. She warms up a bottle, and I sit and feed him.

"I think I'm going to go to church," I suddenly blurt out.

She smiles. "You don't say…"

"What do you think?"

"I think church is important to Tag, even if he doesn't want to talk about it right now, so it's probably a good idea."

"I saw one on the corner, and since it's Sunday…"

She nods. "Okay. Let me change my clothes and I'll join you."

My heart squeezes at the very idea that she'll go with me.

"It's non-denominational," I say. "Do you think it matters?"

She pats the top of my head as she walks by. "I think what matters is what's in your heart, mija."

Tears prick the backs of my eyelids and I don't even know why.

Marta comes back out just as Benji burps loudly in my ear.

"You ready?" she asks.

"You sure you want to go?"

"I'm positive," she says.

Well, I'm not completely positive, but I think this is what Tag needs. And I'm going to try to give it to him.

I grab Benji's bag just as Peck comes in to feed Sammy. She takes him and sits down. We tell her where we're going and she stares hard at me for a long moment. Then she nods. "I'll join you there as soon as I get him fed."

I feel like I'm going to cry all of a sudden.

Marta and I walk down the street together, and I feel solemn and resolute as we enter the church doors. We slide into a pew and I let the feeling of church wash over me.

I hope Tag wakes up in time to join us, but it's okay if he doesn't, because I have his son in my arms and we're in the one place where he needs for us to be.

Tag

Someone shakes my toe and I pull my foot in, but my knee bumps the roof of the bunk bed and I grumble.

"Dude, get up," Sam says. "We need to be somewhere."

"What?" I lift my head. "Where's Finny?" I look around, still trying to get my bearings.

"Get up, dude," he says again. He's staring down at his phone and texting. "We need to go."

"Go where?"

He grins at me like a fool. "You'll see."

I get up and get dressed, and we step out of the bus together.

"This way," Sam says as he points down the street.

"Where are we going?" I ask.

He grins at me again. "You'll see."

Something is up, but I have no idea what.

"So, what's the deal with you and religion?" he asks me.

I shrug, and heat creeps up my cheeks. "No deal. It's just…never mind."

"No, tell me."

Emilio joins us in the street, and he says, "Tell me too. I'm curious."

I jam my hands into my pockets. "When I had nothing at all, and I felt like I was in this dark hole, my faith sustained me. Faith is what's left when everything else has been stripped away."

Emilio nods and claps me on the shoulder. "Good enough," he says.

We walk up the steps of a tiny little church that's a few blocks from the venue, and I can hear organ music playing inside. My heart fills up with love, because religion is the only thing that sustained me for quite some time. I'm still confused, though, about why we're going to church—until we step inside and I see Finny sitting beside Marta in a pew, and she has my son in her arms.

She smiles up at me and it's like my heart cracks open. "What are we doing?" I whisper to her as I slide in beside her.

"We're going to church," she whispers back.

I kiss Benji on the forehead and he kicks his little feet at me. Emilio goes to sit on the other side of Marta, and Sam scoots into a pew behind us. A few minutes later, Peck and their baby join them, and pretty soon the rest of them come too. Star and Josh, and Logan and Emily arrive with their little girl. Emily lays a hand on her pregnant belly and Logan looks down at her, and they don't look displeased to be here. Lark and Wren arrive, and Wren comes and kisses me on the cheek. Then Star shoves the side of my head and I know that we're all right. We're going to be fine.

"Why is everyone here?" I whisper to Finny.

She cups the side of my face and tells me, "This is what family does, Tag."

My heart does that cracking-open thing and I have to wipe my eyes. "But no one here is religious, are they?"

She smiles at me. "Does it matter?"

"I guess not," I say, more to myself than to her.

For the next hour, we listen to a sermon about the importance of being kind, and I watch as Sam and Logan bow their heads during prayer, looking so reverent and earnest, and I'm flummoxed by it all, but it feels right to me.

They do the altar call, and I drag my sweaty palms against my thighs.

"You should go," Finny whispers.

"You want to go with me?" I ask her.

She nods. I take Benji from her and we go hand in hand with my son in my arms to the front of the church. I drop to my knees and Finny kneels beside me and takes my hand. The preacher says a few words and I look over at Finny. "I'm going to ask your dad if I can ask you to marry me," I tell her.

She blinks hard, but she nods. "Okay," she whispers, and she squeezes my hand. "He might say no."

He'd be a fool not to, I think. I chuckle.

We listen as the preacher prays over us, and a sense of peace settles over me. I lost my faith a little when Julia left me and then she wanted to give our baby away. But I've found it again. And it's all because Finny has led me back to it.

"I'd say yes," she whispers, looking at me out of the corner of her eye, her head still bowed.

My heart soars.

Finny

We walk out of the church and find Jason and a few other members of security standing on the steps. He's wearing a cast on his arm, but he looks fit and healthy.

I throw myself at him. "When did you get here?"

"Just arrived. Couldn't let you go to church without me, could I?"

"I'm glad you're back at work." And I really am. He's like family.

He picks up my hand and puts a wad of rolled up money in my palm, then closes my fist. "I never did give you the money you earned that night at the bar. For the homeless."

I had completely forgotten about it. I see the donation box on the wall of the little church, and I shove the bundle of money inside.

Emilio winks at me and gives me a nod of approval.

"That was a beautiful service," Marta says.

I nod. My heart is still in my throat over the way they all showed up at church for Tag. My family is awesome. And some day, I hope he's going to become a even bigger part of it.

Star points off into the distance. "Look, there's a carnival!" she cries. She squeezes Josh's shoulder. "Can we go?"

I can see a roller coaster in the distance, and a Ferris wheel—and my heart stops.

"You guys go ahead," Tag says. His hand squeezes mine. "We'll go back to the bus."

"Come with us, Finny," Star says. She looks from me to Tag and back.

"We can go," I say quietly. I step onto my tiptoes and pull Tag's head down to mine. "I can handle it."

"You don't have to handle anything," he tells me. "We can just go back to the bus."

"I'll take the babies if you all want to go," Marta offers.

I shake my head. "We'll take him with us." I hold Benji close to me. "You guys can come too." I hope they come.

No one but Tag knows about the fair incident with my mother.

He looks hard at me. "Are you sure?"

I nod. "I'm sure. I'll be fine."

We walk hand in hand toward the fairgrounds, and Emilio pays the entry fee for everyone. We buy cotton candy and walk through the fun house, taking time to look at ourselves in the big mirrors, wowing over the way our bodies get distorted. We look at the animals and laugh when Sam steps in cow manure. We ride a few rides, and then we get to the Ferris wheel.

"We're going to skip this one," Tag says. "You guys go ahead."

I square my feet. "I'm riding this one," I say. I will do this. I will not be stuck with a terrible memory for the rest of my life. "I can do this."

Tag stares into my eyes. "You don't have to."

"I do," I say firmly.

Tag passes over tickets for us, and we get into the little car.

I get in and Tag reaches to take Benji from me. "I want to hold him," I say.

He doesn't try to take him from me, but he looks worried.

"I'll keep him safe," I rush to say. "I promise not to let anything happen to him."

The realization of the truth of this settles deep inside me. I have an instinctual need to protect him. I don't know where it came from or how it started, but I would die to protect this kid that's not even mine. My insides suddenly stop roiling quite as much.

The car moves and we go up a bit, stopping as Emilio and Marta get in the one below us. Our family takes up most of the ride, because there are so many of us. Then we start to move. I clutch Benji tightly to me and I don't even realize I'm crying until I feel his little shirt grow damp.

"You okay?" Tag asks.

I nod. The wind blows my hair back as we go around and around, and a sense of peace washes over me. "I think I get it now, Tag," I say.

"What do you get?" He brushes wisps of my hair back from my face.

"*This* is what falling feels like," I say.

He brushes the wetness from my cheeks. "I think I love you, Finny," he says quietly.

"This is what falling feels like," I say again. I lean back against the seat and I know that I would never let anything happen to Benji. I would never torment him or make him hurt, and I know that I could be a good mother to him. "I want to marry you," I say. "Like, really soon."

He grins and looks over the edge of the ride. I look over too. "Emilio," he calls out. Emilio looks up. "Can I have your permission to ask Finny to marry me?"

Emilio looks at Marta and she just smiles at him and nods. He cups his hands around his mouth and calls back, "If you ask her and she doesn't kick you in the nuts, you can take that as a yes!" He grins at me.

I sit back and look at Tag. His eyes are shiny with tears.

"So, are you going to kick me in the nuts if I ask you to marry me?" he says.

I grin at him. "Try me and see."

"Will you marry me, Finny?" He looks down at Benji. "Well, us." He smiles. "We're kind of a package deal."

"I wouldn't have you any other way," I say.

"So is that a yes?"

I feel like my heart is going to explode in my chest. I nod. "It's a yes."

"How are your nuts, boy?" Emilio calls from the bucket beneath us.

"She said yes!" Tag calls back.

Cheers erupt from all around us.

When we get off the ride, Emilio and Marta take the babies and go back to the hotel. We spend a few hours walking around the fairgrounds, with the security team following. There are a lot of curious people who follow us with cameras and I know it's going to take some time for Tag to get used to this lifestyle. We're under constant scrutiny, and even the smallest things are taken out of context.

I tug on Tag's arm. "Can we ride the Ferris wheel again?"

He brushes hair back from my face. "I'll give you just about anything you want," he tells me.

I sigh. "I am pretty sure I'm in love with you."

We kiss, and someone hoots and snaps a picture. "No privacy," Tag grumbles. "Is it always like this?"

I nod and grimace. "Pretty much. You want to go back to the bus?" I silently groan at the thought of the cramped bus.

"Or we could get a hotel room," Tag says. "You could let me hold you all night."

"Would penises and vaginas be involved?"

He grins. "That's totally up to you."

I rest my forehead against his chest and breathe deeply. "I want a room," I say, but I've never been quite so nervous before. I have had sex with a lot of men and never, not once, have I been this afraid.

***

My hands quiver as I unlock the hotel room door with the keycard. Tag follows me inside. Marta had taken Benji from us and wouldn't take no for an answer when Tag protested. I'd slipped my hand into his and told him Benji would be fine for one more night. Tag took a deep breath and let him go.

His hand settles at the small of my back as I walk into the room, and he stops and looks around. "Nice room," he says.

"Yes, it is," I agree. I jerk my thumb toward the bathroom. "I'm going to go and take a shower. Will that be all right?"

He nods and grins. "You need some help?" His dark eyes dilate and grow even darker.

I hide my face by turning away from him. "I think I can manage."

I start to close the bathroom door and he calls my name.

"Finny…"

I look back. "Yes?"

"Why did you take me to church today?" he asks softly.

I shrug. "I just though you needed it."

"I did. I really did." He scrubs his face with his hands and groans. "I haven't had a family in a long time. I think I like yours."

I nod. "They're pretty awesome."

"Can Benji and I be a part of it all?" he asks quietly. "We don't really have anyone else."

I step back out of the bathroom. "What about your uncle?"

"He died last year. Best day of my life." Tag growls low in his throat. "He hated me with a passion."

I sit down beside him. "Why do you say that?"

He shrugs. "I wasn't his son. Since he was our uncle he was obligated to try, though, and he picked me. And through the years, all I could do was thank God that he picked me and not Jessica and Jenny."

"Star and Wren," I correct.

He smiles. "Whose idea was it to get new names?"

I think back. "It started with Peck. Emilio kept calling her the 'fucking woodpecker' because of all her tapping. And then she asked if she could legally change it when she changed her last name. Since she did, we all did. We all wanted brand new starts. Star is the Starling. Wren picked her name because it sounded so much like Jen. And Lark was the last one. Someone told her a lark was a joke *and* a bird, and she loved it. So it stuck."

He turns to face me. "What was your real name?" he asks.

"It doesn't matter. That name isn't who I am anymore."

"You don't want to tell me?"

I heave a sigh. "It was Madelyn. Maddie is what my mom called me."

He stares at me like he's memorizing my features.

"I used to have nightmares about falling all the time. I would wake up in the middle of the night and call out for Emilio. He'd come and grouse around long enough to convince me that no one would dare harm one of his girls or they'd have to deal with him, and that I could go back to sleep because he would always protect me. So one night I told him how I dream about falling, and he said I needed to be a bird because birds don't fall. We looked out the window and saw a finch, and I became Finch."

"It suits you. Still hard getting used to calling my sisters by their new names, though. That might take me some time."

"Secretly, I think they like knowing you're here and that you know their pasts. They love you."

"If I had known about Star and what happened to her…" His voice trails off as he clenches his fists.

I kiss his cheek. "You had no way of knowing." I turn him to face me. "And she's happy now. Really happy."

"She's going to be a mom," he says on a slow exhale.

"Crazy, right?" I laugh. The room goes silent. "Can I ask you something?"

He brushes a lock of hair back from my face. "You can ask me anything."

"How did you meet Julia?"

He scoots back on the bed and leans against the headboard, extending his legs down the length of the bed. He pats his lap, and I lay my head down across his legs with my face up, pointing toward the ceiling. He pulls my hair from beneath me and starts to drag his fingers down the length of it. I stifle a moan because it feels so good.

"When I was nineteen, I met a preacher in our community. He ran an after-school program for kids who didn't have a lot of money or didn't have a good home life or whatever. I knew Julia vaguely from school, and he was Julia's father. Anyway, he offered me a lifeline and I took it." He points to his chin. "When I showed up with a busted chin, he took me to get it stitched. And when I had a black eye, he gave me an ice pack. And he let me talk while he listened, really listened. And he taught me about religion and faith and redemption, and all the facets of religion that were as necessary to me as breathing by this time. When I had nothing else, I still had faith."

"Where is he now?"

"He died right after Julia and I got married."

I jerk upright. "You're *married?*"

He shakes his head quickly. "Not anymore," he rushes to say. "We divorced right before Benji was born."

"Why did you divorce?"

He shrugs. "We were too young, and she wanted to go to college, so she didn't want our baby."

"But she's his mother!"

"Yes."

"But she gave him up…?"

"She did what she thought was in his best interests. She wasn't ready to be a mom."

"Were you ready to be a dad?" I ask.

He nods. "I was. I remember my dad. He was awesome. He tossed the ball with me, and made me put on ties to go to social events. He taught me what it means to be a husband and a father, which was why it was so hard living with my uncle. My uncle was the antithesis of my father. He was evil and mean and he couldn't love anyone."

"And you want to be the kind of dad your dad was?" I lay my head back down on his leg and I feel him go soft under me.

"Yeah, I hope so."

"So what was the money for?"

"Before he was born, Julia had made arrangements with a family to adopt Benji. I was away on the mission trip I told you about, and she didn't have anyone to turn to. The adoptive family promised to put her through college, which is pretty common in adoption situations, particularly when the parents are young. She had her head set on going to school, and she didn't want to give that up. So I promised that I would get the money and give it to her in exchange for Benji. That's why I came to find Star and Wren."

I roll over to face him a little, propping my head on my upturned palm on his lap. "So all that was a setup?" That part still irks me.

"Not really. I mean, I *did* want to see them. But I also needed the money, and they were my only chance."

"You are Benji's father. You shouldn't have had to pay for him!"

He winces. "I know. But I truly did want her to be happy. I loved her."

My gut clenches. "Are you...still in love with her?"

He rocks his head back and forth like he's deciding. "I think part of me will always have feelings for her, but it's not...well...never mind."

I sit up and face him. "It's not what?"

"When Julia and I got married, I remember standing before the Justice of the Peace and thinking to myself, am I doing the right thing? But I did it anyway, because I loved her and I wanted to spend my life with her. But then once we were married, it wasn't what I expected. She was often sullen, and no matter what I did it didn't get better. So I spent all my time trying to make sure she was happy. It was exhausting."

"Then you left."

He nods. "I went on the mission trip with the church, and she fell into someone else's arms and wanted out of our marriage. But by then she was pregnant with my baby."

"If she showed up today and wanted to try again, what would you say?" I hold my breath and wait for his answer.

"I would tell her I'm head over heels in love with his cute little chick named Finny who has filled up all the cracked spaces in my heart."

My breath catches. That's just about the most beautiful thing I've ever heard.

"Do you want to be a mom?" he asks softly.

"I never really liked babies very much," I admit. It's true. No need to hide it.

"Oh," he says. He lets out a heavy exhale.

"But I love yours. So if you're asking me if I could love him like a mother would love a child, the answer is yes. I could."

"Do you ever feel shafted because of your adoption?" he asks.

I snort. "I feel shafted that I have a mother who is mentally unstable. But adoption? No. No shafting there." I take in a deep breath. "Marta has proven to me that a mother *can* love a child who doesn't share her DNA. Without reserve and without prejudice. She's my mom, and I love her and she loves me back. That's all there is to it. I hope whoever you marry will be the same thing for Benji."

I get up off the bed because I'm feeling sort of lost after this conversation.

"Finny," he calls out as I head to the bathroom.

I hesitate, still feeling raw and exposed. "Yes?"

"I know this has gone really fast, but I want to be with you and see where this thing goes."

"I do too," I whisper. I don't know if he hears me or not.

"Finny," he calls again. I turn back, but this time I meet his eyes. "What's wrong?" he asks.

"I'm just feeling really...sad all of a sudden."

"I thought you were happy," he rushes to say as he gets to his feet.

"I am—"

"But you said *whoever* I marry." He bends down so he can stare into my eyes.

"Whoever gets to be Benji's mother will be a lucky woman," I tell him, then I go into the bathroom and close the door.

I turn on the shower and stare at my reflection in the mirror while the water warms. What if I'm not meant to be Benji's mother? What if Tag can never love me like he loved Julia? What if...what if the world keeps turning and I want to get off?

"*This* is what falling feels like," I say to the mirror.

My reflection stares back at me.

Suddenly the door bursts open and I step back in the small bathroom to dodge the bump of it.

"What did you mean when you said that?" Tag demands to know. "Are you telling me that you don't want to be with me?"

"We really just met—"

"We met months ago," he corrects.

"No, we *fucked* months ago," I say.

He freezes. "Is that why I can't get you off my mind? Because it was just fucking? Is that why you gave me what I needed today when you took me to church? Is that why you are in my head and in my heart and so damn deep in my soul?" He pulls me hard against him. "Tell me to go away," he growls.

"I can't," I whisper. Then I draw his head down to mine and kiss him. It's a fear-filled, lust-ridden gnashing of teeth and tongues, and my breath stutters in my chest. I push him back. "I can't think when we do that," I complain. "I can't tell you to go away but I can't tell you to kiss me, either. I have no idea what to do with you."

"Just love me," he says. "Or is that the problem? Am I simply unlovable? If that's the case, just say so."

I cup his face in my palm and stare into his brown eyes. "You're not unlovable. I'm just not sure I'm worthy."

"What?" He covers my hand with his on his cheek.

"What if I'm not good enough to be a wife and a mother?"

"You're good enough. Better than good enough. You're so *much* that you make my heart stop just looking at you." He squeezes my hips. "Then I touch you and I lose all reason."

He clears his throat. "That first night when you pulled your top down and sat in front of me with your tits out and no shame at all, I thought I wanted you then. And when you took me to church and you brought your whole family to support me, I knew I needed you then. When you cried on my son's shoulder on the Ferris wheel, and you held him close and protected him, I knew I loved you then, because that was the most beautiful thing I've ever seen. But now, right this second, I want you and I love you and I can't live without you, Finny. If you tell me to walk away, I will. But please tell me to stay. I understand if you don't feel as strongly as I do yet, but just give me time to make you love me."

"Why did you come to this hotel room?" I hate that I need to know, but I do.

"Because I wanted to hold you all night."

"That's the only reason?"

He looks directly into my eyes. "Yes."

"You had no expectation of sleeping with me?"

He grins. "I *hoped* I would get to sleep with you, Finny, I won't lie. But if you're not ready, I'll settle for whatever you'll give me."

I kiss him then, and he kisses me back. It's soft and tender and slow. Then I turn my back, pull my shirt over my head, and ask him without words to unhook my bra, simply by looking over my shoulder at him. His lips touch my shoulder as he works the clasp. The straps fall away and I let the bra drop over my arms. I kick my shoes off, yank off my socks, push my pants down along with my panties and step out of them. The screech of the shower curtain when I pull it back is loud.

My knees wobble, and Tag palms my naked hips to steady me. I immediately stick my face in the spray, and close my eyes, because his eyes are raking up and down my body and I feel more naked and exposed than I have ever been.

"Are you coming in?" I ask quietly.

Tag

Damn if she hasn't taken my breath away. My knees are weak and my hands are shaky as I take my clothes off. She watches me from the shower, her eyes narrow slits. She picks up the shampoo and fills her palm, and then starts to lather it into her hair. Her eyes close when I get in behind her and draw her bottom back to rest against the tops of my thighs. My dick is so hard I could pound nails with it, but I want to take my time. I want to savor her.

I turn her to face me and pull her hands from the suds in her hair, replacing them with mine. "Let me," I say when she starts to protest. Her hands fall flat on my chest and she lets me suds her hair up, letting out a little moan because it feels good. I tip her head back under the spray and watch the lather sluice down her body, right where my tongue is dying to go.

I kiss her, our mouths melding under the water until I can't breathe. I lift my head and take the spray on my face. Her lips touch the bottom of my chin and she walks up the sensitive skin toward my ear, taking tiny, awesome little nibbles of my jaw. I kiss her again. I can't get enough.

"I need you," I say.

She looks at me.

"I want you," I tell her.

She stares into my eyes, and I can feel her breath hitch.

"I love you."

Her cheeks color. "I need to wash," she says.

I grin. "Don't let me stop you."

"I might need a little privacy…"

My dick is hard between us, and I press it into the notch between her legs.

"Tag!" she cries. "I need to clean up."

I pull back and spin her to face the wall. "Later," I say close to her ear. I draw her bottom back and spread the cheeks of her ass with my thumbs. "Are we safe?" I ask, then I bite down gently on her shoulder.

"Safe?"

"I was tested. Were you?"

She nods, and places her palms flat against the tiles of the tub surround. "Right after you and I… Yes. I was tested."

I want to ask her. I need to ask her. But I won't. I can't. Because it would break my heart to know.

She apparently read my mind. "There hasn't been anyone for me since you, Tag."

"That guy you brought home…?"

"He kissed me. Nothing more."

"Any chance I could get you pregnant?" I nudge at her slick heat with the head of my dick and she sucks in a breath.

"Are you asking for permission to get me pregnant? Or are you ruling out pregnancy as an option?" She looks over her shoulder and laughs at me.

I think about it a moment. "I would love to see you pregnant. With my kid. Our kid. Your belly big and swollen and your boobs full. You'd be full of *us*."

She pushes her bottom back toward me. "Tag—"

"This isn't turning you on, is it?"

"I can't get pregnant. At least not today," she says. "But—"

I freeze. "But what?"

"But I've never done it without a condom. Never. Ever. I'm afraid."

"I'll take care of you, Finny. I promise." I notch my dick toward her heat and wait. "Do you trust me?" I ask her.

"Yes!" she cries.

"Tell me you're ready for this. For me. For us." I wait, poised at her heat.

"Yes!" she says loudly.

I wrap my arm around her waist and surge inside her. She takes me, all of me, and she gasps as I sink balls-deep. Her warm heat wraps around me and holds me, snug and tight.

"Damn, this feels good," I say. I palm her breasts, hefting the gentle weight of them in my hands, and draw her nipples into sharp points with elongated pulls of my thumb and forefinger. "What can I do to make you feel good?"

She takes one hand from her boob and moves it down to her lower lips, and I slide my fingers against her slick skin. She's slippery-sweet and wet, and it's not from the shower. It's from how much she wants me. This. Us. I find her clit and circle it, trying to be gentle, but she covers my fingers with hers and shows me how rough I should be.

"God, Finny," I growl close to her ear, and then I draw her earlobe between my teeth. "I can't wait."

She cups the back of my neck in her palm. "It's okay. Come, Tag."

I pull out of her, her silken heat tempting me to pump back inside, but I can't. I have to give her pleasure.

I spin her around and push her back against the wall. Then I drop to my knees in front of her, lift one leg over my shoulder, and I lick her wet slit, quickly finding her clit and drawing on it with the suction of my mouth. She lays her head back against the tiles and closes her eyes. Her hips rock in time with my tongue and I know she's close. I slide two fingers into her silken sheath and she cries out. Her fingers tangle in my hair and she jerks it.

"Sorry," she says. "You don't like that, do you?"

I take her hands and bury them in my hair. *Show me how much you want me, Finny. Guide me. Love me so I can love you back.* She tugs, and I find a rhythm in time with her hands. Her vaginal wall squeezes around my fingers when she comes, and I lick her over and over, her body shuddering and quaking as I wring every drop of her orgasm from her, until she stills and pushes my head away.

"My turn," I say. I lift her up and she wraps her legs around my hips as I sink inside her. She's so hot and so sweet, and I know I'm going to shoot my load, so I push her back against the tiles so that I can thrust harder. I need to take her. I need for her to be mine.

"Make me come like this," she says.

"Tell me how," I say. I kiss her, covering her cries with my mouth, taking them inside me as fuel.

"Harder, Tag!" she urges. I hook my arms beneath her knees and hold her up so I can pound into her.

"God, you're so pretty when you come," I say, just as her eyes flutter closed and her spasms start to milk me. I'm on the edge now. "Can I come inside you? Can I, Finny? Can I come inside you? Please say yes. Oh, God, please say—"

"Yes! Do it, Tag!"

I slam hard into her one last time, and I come deep inside her as her orgasm sucks me deeper, farther, and deeper still, until we can't join any more completely. Until I can't do more to fill her up. I have never come so hard, so long, or so powerfully. This woman, she fills me up. And she empties me out. And she makes me whole, while taking a piece of me at the same time. I don't know how to explain it.

"God, I love you," I tell her.

She kisses me, and I ease her legs down so that she can stand up.

"I feel weak as water," she says, giggling nervously.

"Stay there. I'll clean you up."

I lather up a washcloth and begin to clean her all over, when she hisses. "Easy," she warns. "I'm a little sore." So I take special care to be gentle between her legs.

"Did I hurt you?" I stand up and kiss her.

"No," she breathes against my lips. "It was perfect."

I wash my come off of her and clean her up completely, and then I wash myself. I turn off the water and wrap her in a towel, and sling one around my hips.

She turns back the covers on the bed and climbs between the sheets naked, and I slide in behind her, drawing her back so we fit like two spoons in a drawer. "Are you okay?" I kiss her shoulder.

"Yes." She turns her head and kisses the inside of my upper arm, where her head is resting on it. "I'm okay."

I yawn and close my eyes, and fall into an immediate and perfect slumber, with the woman I love in my arms.

Finny

When he's still, I lift up the covers and slide out of bed. I look back when he stirs, and I cover his arm with my hand until he settles again. When he's quiet, I get up and get dressed, pulling on my pajamas and a robe. Then I put on my slippers and go into the hallway.

I know where Marta and Emilio's room is, so I go there and knock softly on the door. I know they're not both asleep because they have two babies with them.

Emilio comes to the door, his hair standing out like a ratty halo around his head. He's bouncing Benji in his arms. "Hey, Finny," he says. "Did you need something?"

He steps aside so I can walk past him. "Not really," I say. The hair on my arms stands up, and I rub up and down them to calm myself. "Is Marta up?"

He shakes his head. "Do you need her?" He tilts his head at me. "Are you all right?"

"I'm fine. I just wanted to talk. That's all."

He points to a chair and falls into the one beside me, still bouncing Benji in his arms. "What's up, Finny?" He stares hard at me. "You better start speaking before I have to go kick that boy's ass." He starts to get up, but I rush to sit him back down.

"Tag didn't do anything," I tell him. My cheeks flush. "Well, he didn't do anything bad."

His brows shoot up. "But..." he prompts.

"But nothing," I say quietly. I shrug.

"*Fuck* but nothing," he barks. "I know you, Finny Vasquez, and I know you have something on your mind, so you might as well spit it out."

Benji is fussing, so I reach for him and take him into my arms. He immediately settles into me and I hold him close.

"Well, I'll be damned," Emilio says. "They finally got you."

I heave a sigh. "Both of them got me, Melio." I stare down into Benji's perfect little face. "I am pretty sure I love them."

He nods. "You got time for your old man to tell you a story?"

"Yes, please." Benji makes a snuffly little noise as he roots around his pacifier. Melio passes me the bottle he must have been feeding him, and I pop it into his mouth. His rosy red lips close around it and he looks so content. So well cared for. So happy.

"Once upon a time, there was this little birdie named Finny," he begins. He smiles at me. His eyes go soft. "And she had these perfect feathers, and a perfect beak, and she was smart. She flew all by herself without even needing to hold anyone's tail feathers. She was always independent, and the daddy bird always worried, because she liked the boy birdies a lot."

I roll my eyes.

"But the daddy bird, he never worried about the Finny bird. He worried more about all the hearts she broke as she jumped from nest to nest."

"I don't think I like this story," I grouse.

"You see, Finny was afraid to stay in one nest too long, because she thought that getting comfortable would make her nest unstable, and she might fall out." He slaps his palms together. "Splat! No more Finny."

"You suck, Emilio."

"But the daddy bird, he knew it was just fear that kept Finny moving from nest to nest, and that when she found the right one, she would be willing to sit in the nest a little longer. The daddy bird worried about some of his other birdies, but never Finny. She was strong and she was true, and she was as reliable as the day is long."

His eyes fill up with tears and mine do the same. "You can stop now," I tease. I wipe my eyes with my sleeve.

He shakes his head. He's not finished yet, apparently. "So while the daddy bird loved and trusted Finny, he always wanted a little more for her. He wanted her to have a nest of her own, but in order for that to happen, she would have to find another bird who would keep her safe from falling."

"The daddy bird kept her from falling," I correct.

"But the daddy bird knew he wasn't quite enough. She needed her own family, and her own birdie to love, and she needed someone to make her feel safe forever." He slams his hand down on the coffee table. "*Bam!*" he cries.

Benji and I both jump. "Damn it, I hate it when you do that," I mumble.

"Bam," he says again, a little more softly. "She runs into a certain boy birdie, and this boy birdie knocks her directly out of the sky. But just as she's tumbling to a tragic death, he reaches out to catch her and he keeps her from falling. But Finny…well, she's slow to trust, so it took some time."

"Melio," I mutter.

"Finny is smart and loyal and kind and loving, and she's all the things a daddy bird could ever want in a baby bird. And I'm damn happy you found Tag, Finny, because that boy loves you and you need him." He nods toward Benji in my arms. "And you'll make one hell of a mother." He looks at Benji. "You'd do anything to keep that little guy from falling."

A hot tear slides down my cheek. "You think I can do it?"

He nods. "I *know* you can. And so do you. So get off your ass and get it done."

I snort out a laugh and sniffle back a tear. "You suck so bad, Melio."

He holds out his arms. "Here, give me that little one so you can go back and fall in love some more."

I shake my head. "I think I'll take him with me, if that's okay with you." I look up at him and I see pride in his eyes.

"If you think that's best," he says.

"Hey, Melio?"

"Yes, Finny?"

"Did you love me less because I wasn't yours?"

He shakes his head quickly and barks out a laugh. "You were mine from the minute I laid eyes on you, dummy." He gets up and kisses the top of my head. "I'm going to bed before the other rugrat wakes up."

I laugh. "Thanks, Melio," I say. "I love you."

"I love you too, Finny."

I get Benji's bag and take him and his things with me down the hallway, and let myself into the room.

Tag stirs and looks over. "What's wrong?"

"Nothing," I say. "I wanted to get Benji and bring him in here. You don't mind, do you?"

He smiles into his pillow. "Mind? I love it."

He gets up and helps me set up a portable crib for him, and we slide it into the open walk-in closet space. I pull the door almost closed so I'll still be able to hear him, and I can almost see him. He'll sleep for a couple of hours now, I think.

"Thank you for going and getting him," Tag says. He surprises me when he pulls my pajama top over my head and shoves my pajama pants down to my ankles. I step out of them.

"I'm guessing you want me naked, huh?"

He grins and pulls me back to bed with him, spooning us together again. I feel him pressed hard against my backside, and he nudges and slips inside me.

"We have a baby very close by," I remind him. But I'm already arching, trying to take him deeper.

"There won't be a time when there's *not* a baby very close by, Finny," he informs me. He shoves the covers down and rubs a circle right in the center of my ass cheek. Then he lifts his hand and slaps me.

"Did you seriously just *hit* me?"

"Yep."

I laugh. "You got some balls," I whisper.

"Almost as big as yours," he replies. "I love you, Finny." He pulls out of me and rolls me to my back. He slides inside me, pressing so deep that he pushes me forward in the bed.

"I love you too," I say on a moan, because he feels just right inside me.

Sated, we're still sticky with sweat when we hear Benji wake up. He starts to fuss, so Tag gets up and brings him to bed to lie between us for a while. I play with his feet and he kicks his little toes. "He's so perfect," I breathe.

"So are you," Tag says.

He leans over Benji and kisses me, and nothing ever felt quite so right.

Epilogue
Tag

Finny jumps into her jeans, tugging them by the waistband as she hops into them. "If you don't get moving, I'm going without you," she warns. She glares at me, but her eyes are still hot from what we were just doing. She tips her wrist to look down at her watch. "I told Lark I'd be there five minutes ago."

I prop my head up in my palm and look at her. "Tell me again why we're going to the tattoo shop?"

"Because I'm going to have 'Tag is a horny asshole' tattooed on my ass," she tosses back. She rolls her eyes and shoves my arm so that my head falls. "Get up!" she barks.

I really can't help that I'm making her late. It's not often that we have someone watching Benji during the day. We both had the day off today, so Marta volunteered to watch Benji for us. Then one thing led to another, and we ended up in bed the whole morning. She just remembered she promised to go with Lark to the tattoo shop.

I grin at her, but I get up to start getting dressed. "Did you tell me why we're going? Or did I miss that part when you were stripping my clothes off?"

She shakes her head. "I didn't tell you. It's not my secret to tell. It's Lark's."

Okay, now I'm really curious. "But–"

She points her cute little finger at me. "If you're not dressed in two minutes, I'm kicking you in the nuts."

I laugh, but now I know she's serious, so I finish getting dressed and brush my teeth and hair. I try to tame my cowlick, but Finny doesn't seem to mind it. I vaguely remember her holding on tightly to that lock of hair this morning while I ate her out. She has a thing for pulling my hair. I don't mind, because I have a thing for smacking her ass.

She also has a thing for loving me, and I don't mind that either.

I don't know where I'd be right now if I hadn't met her. I was pretty lost when I came to town a few months ago, and I fell right into her bed, and she fell into my heart and into my mind. She burrowed right down in my soul and I don't want to ever let her up for air.

Last night, I woke up to find her side of the bed empty. I went to look for her to be sure she was okay, and I found her standing beside Benji's crib, watching him sleep. She had her hand on his back and she was counting the number of times his chest went up and down.

I walked up behind her and wrapped my arms around her. She leaned into me the way she always does, and rested the back of her head on my chest. "This is what falling feels like," she said to me. Then she turned in my arms and kissed me, and I agreed with her. It's like falling over and over, every single day.

For Finny, falling has turned into a good memory, and we make a new one each day. Every time I see her, I fall over and over. If anyone had told me I'd choose to fall on purpose, I'd have called him crazy.

Finny has become a mother to my son. She's agreed to be my wife, although we still haven't set a date yet. She's my everything. With her and Benji, I can do anything.

I've been working for the Reeds managing their apartment building, and we moved into an apartment there a couple of months ago. We have our own space, and we love having other people with kids nearby. There's always one or another of the Reeds around, or their offspring, or their wives. Life around here isn't boring, that's for sure.

I walk into the living room, and find Finny standing with the front door open and she's waving me forward. "Your nuts are in so much trouble," she mutters at me as I walk by her.

I grab her and pull her against me. "You know you wouldn't do anything to hurt me," I say. I kiss her and she melts against me.

Her hand inches down to my waistband, and then I feel her grab my balls. I freeze. She squeezes a little too hard for comfort. "Finny," I warn.

"I do love you, but I hate to be late," she says, her lips still touching mine. Her grip turns to a caress, and I pull back as soon as she sets me free. One, because I'm getting hard again. And two, because she's in a mood.

She turns to walk in front of me, so I slap her ass hard enough to make her yelp. "Teach you to fake harming my family jewels," I mutter at her. I adjust my junk and get in the elevator with her. She glares at me from the opposite wall, but there's a smile behind her eyes. And heat. And love. Always love.

"Did you talk to Julia last night?" she asks as we step out onto the street.

I nod. "I did."

"And?"

"And what?" I jam my hands into my pockets.

"And you had better tell me what she had to say," she snaps at me.

I grin. "She said she's coming over this weekend. She wants to take him to the park."

Julia called us when Benji was about two months old. She wanted to see him, and I was completely against it. But Finny talked to her, and she felt like Julia was sincere in her desire to be a part of Benji's life. She doesn't want custody, and she doesn't want to even take him for a night here and there, but she does want to see photos and she wants to visit him whenever we'll allow her to. This weekend, she's going to take him to the park for a few hours.

Finny rubs my arm. "He'll be fine," she says. "Kids need their parents' love." She looks sad all of a sudden. "Trust me."

She hasn't seen her own mother in a month. Every time she visited, the violence escalated. It wasn't just against her; it was against everyone. They're trying new meds, and it's helping somewhat, but Finny isn't going back until she can do so safely. Or at least I hope she's not. I'd love for her mother to get better, just for Finny's sake, but I'm not sure it's going to happen.

Finny did decide to go to counseling, though, and she's dealing with the memories of her mother, and the future with her mother, the best way she knows how.

Lark is standing on the sidewalk glaring at us when we come around the corner. "You're late," she says.

Finny jerks a thumb in my direction. "Blame Tag. He's insatiable."

"Eww," Lark says and then fakes some hurling.

I laugh and open the door for them.

We step into the tattoo shop, and Lark runs straight into the new tattoo artist. He catches her by the shoulders and steadies her, and silently asks with his eyes if she's okay. His brows arch and she nods. He lets her go and she adjusts her clothes. Her face is bright red.

Finny's eyes meet mine and she grins.

The new artist's name is Ryan Shepherd, and I met him two weeks ago when they had a "welcome to the Reed Brothers" party. Ryan is an artist from NYU, and he went to school with Logan. He's really good at what he does, which is putting permanent art on people's bodies. He's also profoundly deaf. Finny and all her sisters can sign, so they can talk freely with him, but me…not so much. I'm set up to take a class starting next week. It's hell being the only one in a family who can't speak the language.

Paul Reed walks out of the back of the shop, along with his wife Friday. "Look who's here," Friday says. She looks at us and then at Lark. "What can we do for you?"

Lark plays with a loose string on her long gloves. "I want to get a tattoo," Lark says. She looks down at her feet instead of at them.

"Did you have something in mind?" Friday asks.

Lark leans over, cups her hand around her mouth and speaks in Friday's ear. And damn if the curiosity isn't killing me.

Friday's eyes skitter briefly toward Lark's gloves and then she winces. "Oh, I'm afraid I can't do that. That kind of application is an art all by itself." She looks at Ryan. "Ryan can, though." She waves her hands around until he looks at her. "Lark wants to consult with you about a tattoo," she says, talking and signing to him at the same time.

He signs something back.

"Why you?" she repeats. "Because you're fucking awesome at what she wants."

His eyes rake down Lark's body from head to toe, and I see sweat sheen her forehead.

"Maybe we should come back another time," I murmur to Finny.

Finny glares at me. "Do you know how much courage it's taking for her to do this?" she hisses at me. "Shut it." She draws a hand across her throat like she's cutting her neck. I'm pretty sure she meant that for me.

Ryan signs something.

"How the fuck am I supposed to know?" Friday tells him. She points to Lark. "Ask her."

He throws up his hands.

Friday picks his hands up and holds them in front of him like she's getting him ready. "Talk to her. She might even talk back."

He signs something really quickly.

Friday rolls her eyes. "Yes, she can sign, dumbass."

He signs something at Lark and she smiles softly at him. He mouths it at the same time, and I'm guessing he asks if she signs too.

She holds her finger about an inch from her thumb and nods hesitantly.

He motions her toward the back of the shop and she follows him, her head bowed and her steps tentative. He pulls a dark curtain around them, and my protective instinct goes into overdrive.

"Should we go with her?" I ask nobody in particular. I start in that direction, but Finny grabs my elbow.

"Let them be," she says.

"Why exactly are we here?" I ask.

"Moral support," Finny says.

Paul pulls up a chair and straddles it backward. "Who did that tattoo on your leg?" he asks me.

I look down at the back of my calf. I have an old-fashioned cross there. I got it when I was twenty. "Just some guy in a tattoo shop," I reply.

He snorts. "Just some guy in a tattoo shop, huh?"

I nod.

"You should let me hook you up," Paul offers. "Anything you want. My last appointment just cancelled."

Friday raises her hand. "I'm free too." She looks at Finny. "I could fit you in."

She grins. "Hell yeah." She goes with Friday to the other side of the shop, and they start to talk about designs with their heads together.

"So, I have an idea," I tell Paul.

He grins at me. "You don't say."

He and I sit down together while he sketches something up.

"That's it," I say, when he has it right. Friday has to come and approve it, but I make her promise not to tell Finny what it is. And Finny won't tell me what hers is. We sit on opposite sides of the room, and Friday works on Finny while Paul works on me.

"Do you think Lark is okay?" I ask, looking toward the back of the shop. "Shouldn't we go check on her?"

Paul grins. "She's fine."

"I think he likes her a little too much. Did you see the way he was looking at her?"

Paul chortles. "You don't have to worry about that one."

"Why? Is he gay?" I ask. Now I'm confused.

Friday laughs from the other side of the shop. "God, no. He's straight. But…" She lets her voice trail off.

"But what?" I ask. I wince as Paul hits a particularly sensitive spot.

"He only dates deaf girls," Friday tells me.

Well, that's not what I expected to hear. "Why?"

"He was born into a deaf family. Deaf parents. Deaf grandparents. He only dates deaf girls."

"Oh." Why doesn't that make me feel better? "Are you *sure* she's okay?"

"Oh, for heaven's sake," Friday cries out. She sets her machine to the side and stalks to the back of the shop on those super-high heels she wears. She jiggles the curtain to let them know she's there. Ryan pulls it to the side and invites her in. She's only gone for a minute or two but when she comes back, she's blinking back tears. She clears her throat. "She's fine."

"You promise?" Finny asks. She grabs on to Friday's forearm and makes her look at her.

"I *promise*," she says. Her voice is raw and abraded.

"Okay." Finny releases a sigh and Friday gets back to work.

Everyone is quiet until Lark comes out of the back of the shop. "That's all we can do today," she says. She has her gloves pulled up to her elbows but I can see clear plastic wrap extending from the sleeve on one arm.

Ryan follows her out and squeezes Lark's shoulder. She smiles back at him.

"So, what's Ryan like?" Finny whispers.

Lark looks at him again. "Don't talk about him like he's not here," she says, and she signs while she talks. Her cheeks flush. "And he's very nice."

He grins at her, but doesn't sign anything.

Finny looks at me and holds a finger to her lips. Apparently I'm not supposed to make a comment about how the two of them are looking at one another.

"What are you guys getting?" Lark asks.

She comes over to look at mine. Mine isn't quite finished. Paul still has to shade it in.

"Oh…" she breathes.

Then she goes to look at Finny's and does the same thing.

"You guys are so meant for one another," she says on a giggle. "You even got them in the same places on your bodies."

Finny gets done first, so she comes to let me see her new ink. She had it put on her upper shoulder, right where I like to kiss her the most.

"It's you and me and Benji," she says. "You guys are my heartbeat. Even more important to me than my music, and I've had a love affair with music for a very long time."

She leans over to look at the spot Paul is working on. "Can I see yours?"

Paul sits back so he can show her. It's not quiet done yet, but it's close enough.

"Wow," she says. She kisses me, and I know she loves it as much as I do.

"It's always going to be me and you and Benji."

"Unless maybe it'll be me and you and Benji and...one more..." She lets her voice trail off.

My heart starts to thud. "Are you...?"

She holds up her hands to stop me. "Oh, God, no. It was just an idea..." She waits with a wince on her face.

"A really *awesome* idea," I tell her.

"Friday left room for another name," she says. She grins at me and kisses me again.

I would like nothing more than to marry her and have more kids with her, particularly now that I have the means to support her.

"I can't run a machine with you two kissing over it," Paul grouses.

Finny sticks out her tongue at Paul and goes to talk with Friday.

Lark's stomach growls loudly. "I'm hungry." She lays a hand on her belly.

Paul chuckles. "You better get some food, because he can't leave yet."

Lark looks at Ryan. "You want some lunch?" she asks, signing while she talks.

He shrugs and gets to his feet as if to say, *Why not?*

They leave together, and Finny and I look at one another and grin.

"He doesn't date hearing girls," Paul says again. "It's his rule."

Finny laughs. "I had rules too. I think we broke all of them when Tag and I got together."

"Don't get your hopes up," Paul says.

But he's grinning, too. And Friday…well, she looks like she's plotting.

"Stay out of it, Friday," Paul growls.

She turns her back to him and ignores him, which I think is normal for her. Paul pretends to complain, but inside I think he's grinning too.

And so am I.

More from Tammy Falkner

Tall, Tatted, and Tempting

Smart, Sexy, and Secretive

Calmly, Carefully, Completely

Just Jelly Beans and Jealousy

Finally Finding Faith

Reagan's Revenge *and* Ending Emily's Engagement

Maybe Matt's Miracle

Proving Paul's Promise

Only One

Beautiful Bride

Zip, Zero, Zilch

Christmas with the Reeds

Good Girl Gone

While We Waited

www.ingramcontent.com/pod-product-compliance
Lightning Source LLC
Chambersburg PA
CBHW071905220626
47052CB00002B/217